from

Julian Fane

3 June 1999

Evening

BY THE SAME AUTHOR

Morning
A Letter
Memoir in the Middle of the Journey
Gabriel Young
Tug-of-War
Hounds of Spring
Happy Endings
Revolution Island
Gentleman's Gentleman
Memories of My Mother
Rules of Life
Cautionary Tales for Women
Hope Cottage
Best Friends
Small Change
Eleanor
The Duchess of Castile
His Christmas Box
Money Matters
The Social Comedy
The Collected Works Volumes I and II

Harlequin Edition

Three Stories of Boyhood
Secrets of the Confessional
A Reader's Choice
A Writer's Life for Me
How to Publish Yourself
A Bad Experience
Mistress of Arts

EVENING

Julian Fane

Constable · London

First published in Great Britain in 1999
by Constable and Company Ltd
3 The Lanchesters
162 Fulham Palace Road
London W6 9ER

ISBN 0 094 79550 9
Set in Linotron Palatino 11pt by
SetSystems Ltd, Saffron Walden
Printed in Great Britain by
St Edmundsbury Press Ltd
Bury St Edmunds, Suffolk

A CIP catalogue record for this book
is available from the British Library

To my sister

JUNE HUTCHINSON

Contents

The Summons

It arrived out of the blue, and I wished it had not.

I had retired, was past retiring age, my work was done, and we had at last moved out of London and were still settling into our new home. An invitation that looked like an order, with bribery thrown in, that was not far removed from bullying, was unwelcome and in various senses unacceptable.

The envelope with its foreign stamp had aroused interest at our breakfast table. Neither of us would have objected to a remunerative offer to translate a book of mine into French and publish it in the smartest of all paperback styles. But then I read the letter and passed it across to Grace, who first exclaimed, 'Oh no!' and secondly inquired, 'What do you think?'

The mildest of my thoughts were that I had never been keen on travelling and was not going to sweat out to foreign parts for anyone or anything. I no longer needed to kowtow to a representative of the literary establishment, let alone a fellow-scribbler who had been more successful than I ever was and was certainly richer, but must be in his dotage. Moreover, if he still had enough gumption to summon a stranger to the South of France to discuss a literary project, why had he not had the courtesy to sign his name: who was the character called Curry who signed the letter on behalf of Sir Gerbert Aucott?

My wife put my own immediate response in a nutshell with her exclamatory groan: 'Oh no!'

I believe I can assert without false modesty that she had a vested interest in keeping me at home. Although unliterary folk may not see what I'm driving at, I record with sympathy that she had been married to a writer of a particular sort for many years. My point is that the sort of writer I was needed a relentlessly quiet and regular life on a pretty well permanent basis – social intercourse kept to a minimum, abbreviated holidays, an ascetic diet and much solitude. I was the opposite of Turgenev, for instance, not only in terms of talent but also in my approach to the work we both did: apparently he wrote his books in a few weeks after months of leisurely gestation. Grace had put up with me or with it nonetheless – with my application of her nose as well as mine to the grindstone. She was cooperative, indulgent, supportive, uncomplaining and, she gave me to understand, happy. I was happy and she said with generous conviction that she was. But gradually an idea had moved from the back of both our minds to the front, and become a promise and a plan. One day, God willing, we assured each other, I would write the last chapter and relax the discipline, we would say farewell to bloodstained first drafts and successive revisions, to publishers, proofs, critics, and to London where the rats mostly raced, and in our rural haven recreate ourselves.

'Oh no!' she exclaimed, referring to the possible reintroduction of business as usual.

We were sitting at the table in the kitchen of our new home with its view of the estuary and ever-changing marine climate that lent rays of hope to the worst weather. We had companionable houses clustering round and the theatre of the streets to entertain us. We had not finished unpacking. We had postponed the daunting tasks of hanging our pictures and shelving our books in order to catch the truant sunshine of spring and explore the countryside. Instead of writing for five hours every morning and for two more hours after tea, I played. Grace approved of everything, and so did I. But Sir Gerbert's invitation spoilt our sport.

He invited me to stay in his villa at Cap Ferrat. He wished to offer me the opportunity of a lifetime, he had the cheek to claim – he somehow knew that in a literary context I was at a loose end. The envelope with the French stamp held more than the typewritten letter signed by the Curry person – a single Club Class airline ticket from Heathrow to Nice and a money order for five hundred pounds. If I were to make the mistake of turning down the job, the money order was meant to take care of my return journey and my trouble. The last sentence packed the punch: the fee for doing all I would be asked to do was ten thousand.

Grace was quicker in the uptake than me, her decided negative became a doubtful query.

One of my answers was to damn the man. He mentioned a week's stay, but I saw our whole future compromised. He was poisoning us with a breakfast of predicament. Supposing I were to overcome my antipathy to travel and other scruples and objections, I was bound to be asked to undertake a literary chore or hack work; and supposing I were to agree to perform said chore I would be stuck with yet another book to write, the commitment could be open-ended, I would have compromised my reputation for independence and integrity, contradicted my farewell to the literary scene, and more importantly broken my word to Grace and disappointed the two of us. On the other hand our 'relocation' – modern jargon for moving house – had made the usual mockery of my estimate of costs, our financial cushion to fall back on was reduced to near the point of inadequacy, ten thousand pounds would be a great help in all too conceivable emergencies, and to have said 'No, no' to a payment beyond the dreams of the majority of scribes, indeed a sum of money twice as big as my most remunerative book had earned, might well be to saddle us and myself in particular with a burden of regret liable to grow heavier as time passed and health deteriorated.

Consequently the next question, following on from Grace's, was: 'What shall we do?'

Crystal, our dog, released us temporarily from the grip of indecision. She is a German Shepherd Dog, four years of age, a canine beauty in her prime, not one of those pathetic cousins of hers with deformed hindquarters bred to please English judges at dog shows but a healthy animal, and possessed of a temperament reliable, equable, affectionate, devoted and above all sensitive. Her faults are hard to find: she is a trifle shy with other dogs and apt to hide behind Grace's skirt, metaphorically at least, and she succeeds with difficulty in not showing jealousy of our interest in canine acquaintances. She is amazingly strong, and in equal measure gentle. She lives to win our approval, and vice versa for that matter; and I am convinced she would happily die in order to protect us. She belongs to Grace, but is careful not to exclude me from their mutual admiration society.

Crystal reminded us that she was due for her morning walk. Dogs are the most accurate time-keepers, even if inclined to try to persuade people that their dinner is being served late. They are also noted for their responsiveness to the moods of their owner or owners. But ours shows at once her sensitivity and her exceptionally sympathetic nature by attempting to comfort and console us if need be. She now stepped out of her big kitchen basket, stretched, yawned, approached tactfully, as it were on tiptoes, and, having gazed with her steady brown eyes into Grace's, rested her gold and black head on her mistress's lap. Grace, characteristically and in her turn, not wanting the dog to worry, adjusted her voice so as to reassure and promised that we would all go out soon: whereupon Crystal achieved both her objectives by evincing signs of a joy that was to some extent infectious.

I do not subscribe to the Walt Disney theory of animal behaviour – Crystal is not one of us. She is our best dog, we have never had a better, but she belongs to a different species and behaves accordingly. She nevertheless rewards us for loving her by suggesting that our friendship is at least as close and complete as the human kind.

At ten o'clock that morning we drove on to the moors and walked through sunshine and shadow. It was February, breezy, chilly, yet the air had the almost undetectable and infinitely sweet scent of regeneration. Creeping plants beside the path dared to hint at greenery, and an occasional songbird clinging to a twig seemed to be clearing its throat. Crystal bounded over the springy turf, hunting for something to hunt, then returned as if with broad smiles to keep us company and slink and bounce along at Grace's heels.

She not only shared her joy with us, or rather reminded us that we too had reason to be discreetly joyful: she was delivering a mute parable on the subject of freedom. She was free although she wore a collar with our name on it round her neck and had been on the leash and would be again, she felt free, she was telling us that freedom could be considered a state of mind, and even pointing out that in the last resort we were free to live or die.

Perhaps, therefore, she played a part in the following conversation.

Grace said: 'We could do without that money.'

'We could,' I agreed.

'You're asked to stay in France for how long?'

'A week – seven nights.'

'I wonder if I can spare you for seven nights.'

'Ditto – and you're not invited – which is another bit of bad manners – so I don't see why I should answer the letter.'

'Won't you have to return the ticket?'

'Maybe – but since I'm treated as no better than a ghost-writer, I'm surely at liberty to act like a ghost.'

'I can't help being curious. What do you think he wants you to write?'

'At his age it's unlikely to be any good. But I'm not prepared to take the trouble to find out. If I got there I very much doubt that I'd be able to leave at once, as he says I could. It'd be churlish when he's paying me five hundred quid for a ticket that might cost a hundred and fifty. No – it's a week or nothing, and God knows how many more trips to Cap Ferrat and how many months or years of hard slog if I were to accept his offer.'

'I could stand all that – I promise I wouldn't cut up rusty if you wanted to go and see what's involved – I never quite believed you'd be able to stop writing – and I'm only happy when you're happy.'

'Well – my "ditto" meant that I'm certain I haven't time ever to be parted from you, especially not for the sake of a stranger's shekels. Besides, spring in England shouldn't be missed by choice by a man in my situation. Sorry, darling – I hate talk of anno domini, but it has a bearing because I retired partly in order not to make a fool of myself in print, and I'm far from sure I could do better with somebody else's book than I could with another of my own. Thank you for not packing me off to bring back a load of daily bread.'

'And Crystal and I say thank you for not deserting us.'

'What a relief to have decided to do damn all!'

'By the way,' Grace wound up our discussion, 'who exactly is what's-his-name?'

Of course she knew he hailed from Grub Street, the smart rich end of Grub Street not the slums where writers starve in garrets – his was a household name. But he belonged to an older generation than mine, and I personally thought he must be dead because he had written nothing of note to my knowledge for years.

Grace and Crystal and I drove home, and I prepared to answer Grace's question. That is to say I spent an unaccustomed hour in my study, and I spoke on the telephone to my literary agent and a couple of well-informed friends. Later in the day we strolled down to the local library, where I was able to dig out a few more details and borrow a copy of *Self Portrait*.

My new study is a glorified cupboard on the half-landing of the staircase of our cottage. It might have been designed to discourage my peripatetic method of composition: there would be no room for me to pace about between writing potential sentences. The available space is given over more to books than to a writer of books – we have had shelves installed on most of three of its four walls. The fourth wall has a window with a view of television aerials and chimneys, and a rickety little desk under the window together with an uncomfortable bentwood chair. What I believe they call a 'husband's' telephone stands on the desk – it has a number of its own and can be used when the 'wife' is talking to her friends on the household line; also an adjustable reading lamp.

At the time in question the majority of my books were on the floor, stacked or still in cardboard boxes. But other writers, amateur as well as professional, will understand that I could not bear not to be within reach of my dictionaries. I had rescued and placed them close enough to the desk and the lamp: the dictionary with its discoloured hardback that attested to the services it had rendered me while I wrote my last books – modern, not yet out of date, and scarcely larger than pocket-size so that it would not tempt me to employ uncommon words; and bigger dictionaries for double-checking in, and other dictionaries of quotations, surnames, proverbs, rhyming, dates, foreign languages, and national biography. My dearest indispensable *Thesaurus* was also there, and classical dictionaries, and companions to the literature of the world, and guides to spelling and hyphenation, and last but by no means least my *Bible* with its concordance. Then came the encyclopaedias, the long line of my old *Britannica* and the single volume of *The Reader's*, and dilapidated copies of *Burke's, Debrett's* and *Who's Who*.

My would-be employer figured in *Who's Who*, a lengthy entry, and had even squeezed into three lines in the *D.N.B.* In *Burke's Peerage, Baronetage and Knightage* I found him under his coat of arms. My agent and my friends supplied information of different kinds, personal, scandalous, critical, intriguing.

On the day after the day on which his letter arrived I could offer Grace a biographical sketch.

Sir Gerbert Aucott's official date of birth showed he was eighty years old; but in *Self Portrait*, the last of his twenty-odd books and an almost unprofessionally slim volume, he called himself an Edwardian, which would make him a few years older. He drew a similar veil over his nationality: was his father English, and if so why was he the stationmaster at Aberystwyth? And was his mother Welsh, and why then was she a teacher who specialised in English? Aberystwyth seems to have been his hometown anyway, and he refers in passing to a sister by the name of Queenie.

I vaguely remembered the publication of *Self Portrait*, and my agent reminded me of how badly received it was. The critics attacked with the savagery they reserve for authors they have praised and fear they have over-praised in the past. They picked on his arrogance, high-handedness, equivocations, carelessness, and bayed that the book was paltry and its contents cold-hearted. In my opinion, in this instance, they were not wrong. All the same the writing has the two qualities that authenticate literary talent, the rare and indefinable one termed style, and the commoner essential known as readability.

No doubt the talent in question was better at fiction than fact, and bored by the story it was obliged to tell. *Self Portrait* is dedicated to the author's mother, and was clearly meant to repay the debt he owed her. But too many tributes have been written to ambitious frustrated lower-middle-class women by sons who were driven by them to learn and excel and win prizes and become literary lights. Sir Gerbert's originality would have experienced difficulties with the hackneyed material, and he seemed to regain the lost time of his humble origins with distaste and disdain.

His education resembled that of a princeling of a bygone age. He knew his ABC in his cradle and was soon scampering through Boswell's *Life of Samuel Johnson*. School was nearly a relaxation after the regime of lessons he was required to follow at home. Life in the cottage beside the railway tracks tied to the job of stationmaster revolved round his studies. His mother reserved the parlour for his homework and kept the household quiet while he was doing it; she escorted him to his schools before she went on to her place of employment, a private cramming academy, and fetched him from them too; she walked miles to protect him from harm, also to feed him and make sure he did not eat school fare. She fought battles with her better or worse half and probably with her daughter so that her white hope would be and feel he was the centre of attention.

Retrospectively he does take somewhat for granted the privileges of the clever scion of a poor family. Not for him the heartache and homesickness of being packed off to an expensive boarding school at the age of eight, nor the hardships of ancient seats of learning with their historic wrecks of buildings and unjust customs and rites; yet he writes unsympathetically of his parents skimping and saving for his sake, of their wage slavery, of cramped accommodation and the horrors of the privy in the garden, of bad food, dim neighbours, wet holidays and the unremitting grind of scholastic competition. He derides Aberystwyth and provincial Wales, and especially Welsh nationalists trying to speak their hideous and inadequate lingo.

He is not even very nice about his mother. His descriptions of her are objective to an unflattering degree. She is not tall but stringy, not slim but wiry, not shy but gawky, not hard-working but usually exhausted, and so on. He harps on her dowdiness, her rejection of the arts of womanhood and the consequent dissatisfaction of her marriage, her eyesight affected by too much reading, and her insatiable appetite for success, his success which would be her justification and compensation. He does not hesitate to admit that she was a snob and a prig, and the best compliment he pays her, that she was the first of the women who had made him what he was, is ambiguous.

As bad luck would have it, his mother died just before he reaped a bumper harvest of honours at the end of his university career. He refers to her demise in passing, and implies that he was at last able to enjoy the freedom which she had denied his boyhood and youth. Having risen above his social beginnings he met and married a girl of independent means, and they joined in the revels of the 1920s. He records with perverse pride that the swotting caterpillar was transformed into the social butterfly of the next five years, and that he became a womaniser and a wastrel. When his first wife divorced him he found a second, who was more willing to subsidise his rake's progress.

The turning points were threefold. He fell in love with or under the spell of a maternal replacement, who reminded him of the obligations of his intellectual endowment. To please her or himself, he therefore revised and padded out his doctoral thesis, called it *The Roots of English Poesy* and presented it to the public. It was a complete flop, unnoticed, unsold.

Self Portrait has a photograph of the author in his young days as frontispiece. He was good-looking and his looks were romantic, brooding and sensual, but his face also bears the hallmarks of the artist, the eager vitality and the hint of unusual determination. Although he writes of his first failure dismissively – it was not his fault, he blames the establishment – I can imagine the shock it must have been and that it might have squashed him flat. Evidently it had the opposite effect, he was the more desirous of shining on the adult stage of the world, as formerly at home and in school. He was in the rage of unrecognised talent to arrive at the place in the sun he was persuaded and had been promised that it deserved.

He published the first of the books of his *Terrible Trilogy* under the name Gerbert.

He had been baptised Herbert Benjamin. He had signed *The Roots of English Poesy* in academic style H. B. Aucott. To distance himself from that disaster, to mystify and impress, he reinvented his literary persona by naming it Gerbert. The word was ugly but more striking than his initials, and he was probably glad to get away from ordinary Aucott. And its singularity was bound to attract attention in England, although on the continent a single name adopted for professional purposes is nothing to get excited about, witness the French thespians Raimu and Arletty, and Van Gogh who signed his pictures Vincent.

My agent told me that Gerbert had handled his public relations brilliantly, and agents know that writers get nowhere by merely being good. His assumed name titillated critics and magnetised book-buyers as planned, and its historical associations satisfied snobs and promoted still more sales. The first Gerbert to step into the limelight also changed his name, but by lengthening instead of shortening it: he became Pope Silvester the Second, who presided over the Holy See from 999–1003. Nearly a thousand years later my would-be employer borrowed his name, not least because he had been extraordinarily learned and the possible prototype of Faust.

Apparently Gerbert Mark II made out and spread the rumour that his mother had believed his cleverness was not altogether natural, was linked to some external agency, and could be devilish: she had been a Roman Catholic, had brought him up in that faith, known the history of the Papacy and jumped to the nominal conclusion. He claimed nothing definite, but somehow let slip that his pen was guided by a force beyond his control, and that he feared his scholastic superiority had been positively unfair. In terms more veiled as they were more self-serving, the suggestion was that any adversary of his would have to deal with the Prince of Darkness.

He was on reasonably safe ground. Who can tell what the devil gets up to? Both elder Aucotts were dead, and his sister Queenie was married to Steve Cagshaw, a garage mechanic, and preoccupied by motherhood. He seemed to have no other relations and no childhood friend likely to call his abstruse literary bluff.

Perhaps it was all superfluous: the title of volume one of his *Terrible Trilogy* was *Defecation*.

The fact that saddens sensitive souls and depresses polite people is that in art, modern art, nothing succeeds like offence. Nowadays you almost have to offend somebody in order to be noticed by the media or to scratch a living from art. Heterosexuality in exhaustive detail boiled many a literary pot for getting on for a century. Homosexuality is a new seam of gold or maybe silver. The royal family and the Christian God can be reviled for a bob or two and are unlikely to hit back in the law courts. The dead are fair game, scandalous biographies do well with little risk, and extreme violence, sadism, fetishisms and anything else disgusting are always likely to earn a crust.

Gerbert followed in famous footsteps along a well-trodden path. He carried on from where Thomas Hardy and D. H. Lawrence left off, and was imaginative enough to spot the possibilities in his interpretation of the Yorkshire idiom: 'There's brass in muck.' *Defecation* was published in the good old days of British censorship by the Olympia Press in Paris, and went down well in Europe, in Scandinavia in particular. The whole trilogy, *Defecation, Masturbation* and *Penetration,* was first published in the UK soon after *Lady Chatterley's Lover* and made the name of the author and his fortune.

It gave almost maximum offence. It was condemned by churchmen, politicians, doctors, educationalists, do-gooders and even liberals. Consequently the international newspaper industry serialised it, interested parties hyped it by branding it 'terrible', the film rights were bought for millions and bowdlerised movies broke records, Gerbert became a celebrity and a news item, and the public proved yet again how infinitely strong its stomach was and is.

I read or rather skimmed through the three books in their Olympia editions in the war – the army was always short of pornographic reading material. Setting aside the sensationalism, open-mindedness has to admit they are well-written and entertaining. They are works of art of a sort, and vindicated to some extent by their quality and by the argument that all aspects of existence lie within art's province. *Defecation* is an every day story of life in the lavatory. The titles *Masturbation* and *Penetration* say enough about the two texts, which are comparable with Henry Miller's *Tropics* and Anaïs Nin's *Delta of Venus*.

Gerbert published nothing much for several years after writing the trilogy, but was not idle. His reputation as a scholar and a subversive won him commissions from literary editors who have to sell their wares, and he cut an ever more fashionable figure with his scurrilous journalism, his formidable personality, his money troubles and love affairs. He cultivated his sulphurous image of a man above and beyond the conventions, morality and ethics.

The rest of his literary biography is relatively tame. He began to publish a more or less annual novel, as other authors do. That each one bore a girl's name, *Katie, Sukey-do* about an American, *Carmencita, Sieglinde,* for examples, was a somewhat trivial trimming; and the sex scenes in them were not nearly so lewd as those in the latest bestsellers written by women. When the critics assaulted and battered *Self Portrait,* they also tore his previous books to pieces.

They may have been right to find fault with his essay in autobiography; but their inclusive rage and insolence are probably traceable to worldly rather than literary causes.

Gerbert's prestige had kept them quiet for too long. They were naughtily tempted to prick the balloon of his Faustian pretensions. His wealth, his success with women, were not excused in the purlieus of hypocrisy. And to rub salt into the wounds of envy he had recently purchased the indulgence of the establishment with his huge donations to literary charities. The powers-that-be had forgiven his youthful indiscretions in print and elsewhere and welcomed him on to committees, government quangos, prize juries and the customary programmes on radio and TV investigating the death of the novel. As a predictable result, and before too long, the rank outsider of literature, the scatologist and pornographer, the reprobate was rewarded for coming clean and going straight or straighter with a knighthood.

Briefly he had the world or at any rate his world at his feet. His notoriety seemed to have turned into impregnable fame. He soared out of reach of all the jackals snapping at his heels. He was prematurely the grand old man of British letters, and surely whatever he wrote would be treated with respect and rubber-stamped by the paperback companies and the foreign sheep in the publishers' fold.

But he suffered a great fall. He was suddenly no luckier than innumerable other artists inasmuch as the feast of his career became the famine almost overnight. *Self Portrait* could be said to have been the least of it. He was not much better than the common man in that he lost most of his money. He was a gambler, he had been speculating on the Stock Exchange, had made reckless bets in the futures market, and teetered on the edge of bankruptcy.

The story was gloated over in the press and in the covens of the literati. Gerbert knew the score, and did not hang around to be the Aunt Sally of the vengeful. He announced his retirement and betook himself into exile. He had enough money to eke out existence in the South of France, and was rumoured to have received a handout from one of the benevolent funds for indigent authors of which he had been the chairman.

His force was not, however, spent. The global economy took pity on him, and he met his last wife, Valérie something or other. He acquired a house and called it the Villa Valerie, asserting himself as ever by dropping the accent and anglicising her name.

Two decades elapsed. He remained silent, he was an exception to another rule, the rule stating that writers never know when to stop. The Aucotts were rumoured to live in style – he had rebuilt his fortune. In time he could send me a cheque for five hundred pounds, and Mr Curry on his behalf offered me ten thousand more for doing as I would be told.

A potted version of the above formed the basis of further discussion of Sir Gerbert's offer and summons between Grace and myself.

My line was that I should not have bothered to read the man's rotten little book or research his rather squalid history: after all we had established that I was not going to France. I should have written my refusal and left it at that: I would not break my promise to retire, and to be away from home for even a week was simply not an option.

But the truth of the matter was that I had not been able to resist my reference books, and the telephone calls to my agent and others had interested me against my will. The majority of the opinions I sought confirmed my own view that Gerbert was a formidable sham; but he was also extraordinary, everyone agreed, and I was privileged both to be invited to stay in his palace of a house and to be getting so highly paid for whatever it was he wanted me to do.

Moreover, I enjoyed the hours I spent in my new study, my apology for a study, and felt wistful pangs when I remembered that I would never write a book on the cramped desk.

Something else sapped my resolve. In the present circumstances as in the novels I had written, I wanted to know how the story would end. What exactly was Gerbert offering? How had he coped with his years of retirement? What was he like behind the variety of his masks? Again, the temptation of money was hard to resist: I mean not only the fee I was turning my nose up at, but the fascination of the fleshpots. I would have liked to meet a patron who could and would pay a small fortune for my services, and to investigate the possibility that he had sold his soul.

I would not go to France. I rehearsed all the arguments against going. I had every reason to stay put. But I could not fool Grace, and she teased me for not having returned the airline ticket or the cheque.

I did advance the idea of proposing to bring my wife to Cap Ferrat. No, she said, she would not be foisted on the poor old boy however rich he was, nor would she consign Crystal to kennels, nor leave our house empty and at the mercy of burglars and thieves.

Her own idea was tried and tested and had never been found to be bad: wait, she urged, do nothing for as long as we politely and practically could.

More time passed – two or three days – and we heard that Grace's brother Oliver, her only living relation and for that matter mine, had broken his leg.

In other words fate had intervened. Oliver was much older than Grace and a widower living alone at the far end of a cart track in Gloucestershire. His two children – Anne and Juliet – were married and resided respectively in Canada and Australia. He carried independence to eccentric lengths, was a prickly misanthrope with a drink problem and halfway to being a hermit. His doctor rang to tell us he was in hospital, that the fracture had been pinned and was mending, that Oliver was due to be sent home in the near future, and that he should not have to fend completely for himself for the first week of his convalescence: 'Which settles everything,' Grace said to me.

She was fond of her brother in spite of discouragement, and ready to help him. She knew that he and I were not and never would be friends, and had thought of having him to stay in our house while I was out of it.

I was therefore persuaded to make a telephone call to the Villa Valerie. The woman I spoke to understood neither my English nor my French, but at length a nameless man with a young voice and a Welsh accent took over. No, he said, Mr Curry was in conference with Sir Gerbert Aucott. No, he replied to my further question, Mr Curry was Sir Gerbert's solicitor not his secretary, and had flown down from Wales to deal with some legal matters. He then promised to give my message to Mr Curry.

I made numerous arrangements and braced myself for travel – Grace suggested that I might be travelling to the next world – and said goodbye to my dog and my dearest for the umpteenth time. Train fever notwithstanding, I arrived at Heathrow via London, and my flight was less eventful than I had feared.

Devil's Brew

I left Heathrow in a February drizzle of sleet and the odd snowflake, and approached the spit of land that is Nice Airport along a coastline backed by dark green mountains and lapped by a turquoise sea in dazzling sunlight.

The aeroplane had arrived early; as it was not full, passengers could disembark without delay; I soon regained possession of my suitcase, walked through an exit, saw the white Mercedes that I had been told to look out for, and approached it.

A thickset Asian chauffeur in a blue suit and an old-fashioned blue uniform cap was opening a rear door of the car and the lid of the boot. A youth in jeans and leather jacket emerged from the back seat followed by an identifiable solicitor wearing a raincoat and clutching a briefcase. They were clearly as late as I was early and were in a hurry.

I spoke the passwords, 'Villa Valerie?' – and the Englishman greeted me and introduced himself. He was Mr Curry, and flustered – there had been a delay and they had a plane to catch; the youth was James Cagshaw, the grandson of Sir Gerbert's sister and the person to whom I had spoken on the telephone. Was Sir Gerbert expecting me? Yes indeed – and Lee the chauffeur would drive me to the Villa as planned – and he hoped my stay would be pleasant, and was sorry he had to say goodbye.

Smiling and sweating Lee ushered me into the recently vacated back seat of the big car, and we sped silently through a network of roads and on to the dual carriageway running round

Nice's *Baie des anges* – Bay of angels, Bay fit for angels. On the left were more or less grand hotels and blocks of flats, on the right palm trees and the miles of the *Promenade des Anglais* which I had read about with the sparkling Mediterranean beyond. It was one o'clock local time, and as warm as English summer.

Our road led uphill, and I had a view of a beautiful smaller bay with translucent water. Then signs to Cap Ferrat directed us down and over a railway bridge and unexpectedly to an entrance in a high wall with gates that would not have disgraced a royal residence. This road had the railtrack running along beside it, fenced off by strands of wire and a verge of weeds. It was a narrow road, not pavemented and with potholes and litter, and not where I for one would expect to come across elaborate ironwork twenty-five feet high, sporting crests and coronets.

The railed and gated area was guarded by cameras and an entryphone system, and the wall had a roll of razor wire on top. Lee spoke into the entryphone in his unknown language, and someone must have activated the machinery by remote control. We drove between the two gates, which closed with an ominous crash behind us, and through a charming garden or small park.

Isolated palms cast shadows on expanses of mown sunlit bright green grass. The dominant tree, close to the gateway, was a subtropical baobab – it had multiple trunks growing together, enormous girth, shiny magnolia-type leaves, and strings of brown fibres dangling down. Some of the palms were stumpy, others oddly shaped, others toweringly tall and elegant. A sort of mist – or was it mystery? – seemed to cast a spell over the large white house of which I caught veiled glimpses as the drive twisted and turned.

The car stopped. A tubby Asian woman – Mrs Lee – ran out to welcome me with more smiles and with deferential gestures indicating that I was to step indoors: the Lees were Indonesians. Within the dark cool marble-floored hall another Indonesian, the Lees' daughter Marie, a teenage girl wearing a white nurse's overall, presented me with a sheet of paper unfolded.

Gerbert himself had written on it shakily: 'How do you do? My apologies for not greeting you, and I must also apologise to you for the absence of my dear wife. I hope to be able to meet you at six p.m. in the library. My staff will provide luncheon and be happy to serve you as required – fortunately the Lees excel at sign language. My home, garden and car are at your disposal, and I am told there are worthwhile walks hereabouts. *A bientôt!* P.S. I did not put this note in an envelope since its bearer is illiterate.'

When I finished reading, Mrs Lee beckoned me towards the marble staircase and Lee carrying my suitcase shooed me up the stairs. They showed me my bedroom and adjoining bathroom, and by pointing at wristwatches and mouths they explained that lunch would be ready in a quarter of an hour. In response to my signals that I wished to make a telephone call, a mobile was unhooked from the belt encircling Lee's trousers and handed over with yet another respectful bow.

I rang through to Grace to say I was safely installed.

What was it like? Indescribable, I replied – romantic, exotic, grand, opulent. And mine host? He was either indisposed or resting, anyway invisible, and the wife who lent her name to the Villa was elsewhere; but he had warned me that he would be coming out to play at six o'clock. What was I meant to do until then? Well, I said, I was about to have my lunch cooked and served by two or three servants, and then I might take some carriage exercise and be driven by the chauffeur to the casino at Monte Carlo, where I would stake my all. Seriously, she scolded and laughed, what would I do? Miss her, miss Crystal, miss the comforts of home, and more than likely go to a travel agent to book my return journey.

In the interests of the strictest truth I had to qualify the latter statement – I would wait and see what Gerbert was really like, and for the moment was fascinated by everything. Similarly Grace modified her advice by urging me not to be in too much of a hurry to call it a day.

I descended the stairs and was again taken under Indonesian wings. Mrs Lee produced a three course lunch in the best French style – a plateful of salad, a grilled fish and an apple flan – which I ate under her husband's eyes or rather his teeth bared in smiles. The formal dining-room was sunny despite partially lowered white blinds, chilly nonetheless because of the marble floor. The pictures on the walls were of religious subjects by Italianate painters – the room was stately in the continental tradition, and a most unlikely setting for the kingpin of modern pornos.

Both Lees escorted me to the drawing-room, where I was to drink my coffee luckily and at last alone. Angled sunlight streamed into this room through windows that faced across the bay to Villefranche and the great hill behind it. A fine rug covered most of the marble floor, but the tapestry-covered settees and upright chairs reasserted formality. Double-doors at one end opened into the library, an equally big room that must have faced northwards: it seemed dark after all the light. Here, easy armchairs, occasional tables, reading lights and a desk were somehow a relief. In the floor to ceiling shelves along one wall were copies of Gerbert's books, the *Terrible Trilogy* in numberless editions, hardback, paperback, in recognisable and unrecognisable foreign languages, and those bearing the often absurd girls' names. A complete set of the works, excluding *The Roots of English Poesy* which was nowhere to be seen, had been bound in green morocco, and *Defecation* was inscribed in stylish writing, 'For the author from his loving wife.' No signature or date was appended, and I wondered which of his four wives had been the donor.

The most surprising of my first impressions of the whole place was its dignity. Yes, it was almost palatial and unquestionably monied; yet it avoided the pitfalls of excessive boastfulness, brashness, expat nostalgia, and steered a middle course between luxury and restraint. Could Gerbert have been responsible, considering his cruder literary output and his unsophisticated upbringing? No doubt the Villa was not called Valerie for nothing, and I rather regretted the absence of my hostess, whom I would have liked to compliment on her good taste.

At about three o'clock I thought of taking a stroll in the grounds, but was inhibited by Lee buttonholing me in the hallway and trying to propel me into the Mercedes. I eventually convinced him that I wished to walk, not to be driven, whereupon he smiled wider than ever – possibly more at than with me – and hustled me round a corner of the house and in dumbshow introduced the gardener, his brother. They threatened with the best will in the world to accompany me on my peregrinations, and I hope they were not hurt by my desire for solitude and the discouraging gestures with which I obtained it.

The front door of the house was at the back – I had so far seen only the rear elevation. The opposite side had an extended portico with pillars, providing shade for a table and chairs – this terrace area was accessible from the drawing-room, although I had found the french window giving on to it locked. A wide flight of shallow steps led down to lawn on which longer reclining chairs were arranged under tall pine trees; and there was another terrace at the far edge of the property, balustraded and overlooking the sea.

I stood by the balustrade and compared the panoramic view with my recollections of a map I had studied at home. The Villa Valerie was located on one of the promontories on one of the peninsulas jutting out along the Côte d'Azur. Cap Ferrat with its other dwellings for multimillionaires stretched into the sea on my left hand side. On my right was the perfectly shaped bay of Villefranche, and beyond the hill – Mont Boron – that reared up behind that ancient village lay the city of Nice. The sun still shone on me – the more expensive the property in this part of the world the more it bagged of both the morning and the evening sunshine, whence the great houses higher on the hillsides. The paradox was that trees were then planted, and blinds and shutters installed, to guard against the sun's beams.

I made a couple of circuits of the property, half a mile of walking maybe. Gerbert's quarters seemed to be on the first floor above the library, and the Indonesians to occupy the semi-basement and the lodge by the gates. My return to the house and at length to my bedroom was complicated by having to ring the doorbell and again extricate myself from Lee's clutches. After a brief doze in the blessedly horizontal position on the double bed in my room I spent the hour before my appointment by looking at what could be called the cornerstone of the Gerbert residence, a boxed edition of the first three books that bore his tendentious name.

A literary truism, that today's spiciest chunks of prose are tomorrow's stale buns, applied to them. The titles were good or bad enough, but the obscenities now struck me as dated: pornography has become more pornographic. On the other hand, the enviable style reminded me of the 'line' of a draughtsman of genius, and the tales traced the development of youth by sexological means, an inventive and surely as legitimate a device as any.

Had Gerbert been misjudged by his English detractors, myself included?

I was punctual, but he was waiting for me. He was sitting in one of the easy chairs in the library with his back to the light, not slumped, well-arranged with a tartan rug round his legs. He looked younger than I expected. He had a trim grey beard and had not lost any hair – his hair was thick and short – and his voice was unusual, a light tenor. But he wore dark glasses – what with the lighting, the beard and the glasses I could not see much of him.

'How do you do?' he said and, as if to stop me from trying to shake his hand, added without a pause: 'Take the chair over there if you will.'

He inclined his head to indicate that I was to face him, and I obeyed although I did not like to be literally put in my place – I was not yet working for him.

The epithets applicable to his voice would be silky, melodious. It was certainly not like the voice of an octogenarian, and might have belonged to an actor or singer. His slight regional accent, not recognisably Welsh, lent piquancy to the precise articulation, and the sweet modulations were spellbinding. At the same time his voice was expressive of power, commanding, autocratic, and I felt snubbed by it before I had opened my own mouth.

The blinds that had excluded the afternoon sunshine were

rolled up, and the Mediterranean dusk was falling. Through the window I glimpsed the distant twinkle of a light in a villa on a hill. A single table lamp illuminated the library – the drawing-room beyond the double doors was in darkness. The lamp was bright, it dazzled me and cast shadows across Gerbert's countenance – and I guessed that these effects were deliberate.

We were not alone. I was disconcerted and had scarcely noticed Marie in her white overall sitting motionless and with downcast eyes at the desk, which had been moved to the right – my right – of Gerbert's chair. Marie therefore faced her boss or patient, and incidentally showed me her neat oriental profile and long slim neck. As well as the lamp, two bottles of wine and two glasses on a tray stood on the red leather desk-top.

'You received my note?' I was asked.

'Yes.'

'I hope you're satisfied with your quarters?'

'Thank you, yes.'

'You're not wired?'

'What?'

'You're not recording our conversation?'

'No. No, of course not.'

'Others have tried it, but I threw them out of the house. Dictation has ruined many a good book – dictation was the death of Henry James as an artist.'

'I'd never do anything like that, I can assure you.'

'Do you give me your word of honour?'

'I've given it already – but yes, all right, I do.'

A pause ensued. I was fuming – he had not thanked me for ignoring his rudeness and indulging his paranoia. My goodwill had evaporated, and I contemplated another telephone call to Grace to say I really would be home tomorrow.

'We've never met before, have we?'

'No,' I replied.

'I used to meet too many people.'

'Well, I wasn't one of them.'

'Didn't you belong to any of those corrupt literary societies I made the mistake of mixing in?'

'I was a member of a couple, but, as you may know, I've retired, I don't live in London any longer, and I've cancelled all my literary commitments.'

'Sensible man! Think of Emily Brontë trotting along for tea and a gossip at PEN! Think of Dostoevsky stopping work on *Crime and Punishment* to listen to a lecture on the art of the novel – he did better by losing his wife's wedding ring at roulette! I know nobody gets anywhere unless he's one of the boys; but you're right to steer clear of writers – writers are cannibals to a man – and only a merciful God can save us from the females of the species!'

He relapsed into silence, but seemed to be staring at me through his black glasses. I stared back at him in a vain attempt to detect and interpret his expression. Although age had not destroyed his regular features, it had rendered them rigid – he resembled a statue or waxwork. What was he hiding behind his beard and glasses? He wore an open necked blue shirt and a navy blue cardigan, and his hands were in his lap and covered by the rug.

I was unmoved by the cynical statements – you get used to cynicism in my profession. I could have contributed one of my own by saying that writers should never be taken too seriously, writers of fiction in particular. But I was determined not to plug the conversational gaps and give him another excuse to bite my head off. And I wished I did not feel pleased to have been thrown a scrap of praise.

He spoke again.

'We have company.' He inclined his head ever so slightly in the direction of Marie. 'Have you met her?'

'Yes,' I replied with some force. I did not want him to think that I was as rude as he was and had omitted to acknowledge her existence.

'Do you fancy the back of her neck?'

'No – no comment.'

He was embarrassing me, and I hoped she was unaware of being the subject of his personal remarks.

'The back of a woman's neck goes a long way.' The shadow

of a smile crossed his face – was it lecherous or was he pedantically amused by the peculiarity of his idiom? 'South-east Asia breeds the best – always tell a Korean girl to turn her back! Marie!' His voice dwelt on the name with unexpected tenderness. As if in accordance with a preconceived plan the girl rose to her feet and began to pour red wine into one of the glasses and then the other. Her movements had the grace of unhurried concentration. Meanwhile he was saying: 'But Indonesia takes a different prize. A seductive outline is a joy for ever, but a heart of gold means more to a man of my age. She's a competent nurse into the bargain and stronger than she looks – she doubtless has muscles in all the right places. Don't worry – she doesn't understand a word of English, which suits me – I refuse to waste my declining years in intercourse with domestics.' He challenged me more directly with his next question: 'Are you homosexual?'

'No.'

I was angry again. He was intrusive and intolerable: did I look like a steeper – steeped in the higher philosophy, as Edwardian irony put it? He was a snobbish old chauvinistic billy-goat.

Marie bore the tray of glasses across to where I sat and dropped on to one knee as she proffered it with a fleeting smile before she again bowed her head. I was startled. I might have taken exception to her servility, and had intended to refuse the wine, but I was unwilling to disappoint or treat her churlishly, or to pick a quarrel. I accepted a glass and thanked her for it, and she went and placed the other glass on an occasional table on her employer's left and returned to her chair behind the desk.

He produced a skeletal hand from beneath the rug, grasped and raised his glass to me, and said: 'Here's to your health, but please don't bother to drink to mine!'

I shrugged my shoulders, mentally at any rate, and took a sip. Although I was no wine-bibber and an ignoramus in the vinous line, I had drunk my share for many years, but nothing to compare with that which began to change the complexion of the evening. It was soft and smooth, yet heady. Its mollifying effects were so swift that I suspected momentarily it had been spiked.

'Do you know this coast?' he inquired.

I was later ashamed of replying negatively that I had never been a millionaire and had not frequented any playground since leaving school.

He ignored my sarcasm and asked: 'How do you react to my abode?'

I could not conceal my opinion that it was a marvel, that I had seen nothing like it, that for me it resembled one of those magic houses in classic literary fantasies.

'Valérie is my wife,' he volunteered inconsequentially, giving her name its French pronunciation.

'So I guessed.'

'We changed the name of the villa. It used to be called Céleste, which means heavenly. But it's been heavenly in our days, too. We decided to dispense with the accent – I can't manage frog language.'

His delivery had become ruminative, and I wondered if he was tiring or growing confused.

'She's not here,' he said, 'alas!'

I assumed he was referring to Lady Aucott, and reminded him of his note.

'You won't meet her.'

'So you told me. She has great taste.'

'What makes you think that?'

'Well – the decoration of the house.'

'I had a hand in it.'

'Well – I congratulate you.'

'Do you have a wife?'

'Yes.'

'You didn't bring her with you.'

'She wasn't invited.'

'You could have brought her – she would have been company for you while I was otherwise engaged. Perhaps you're not happily married.'

'On the contrary.'

I held my tongue and kept my own counsel despite the provocation. I refused to discuss Grace and how much I loved her with anyone, least of all this diabolist, to whom I intended to say adieu as soon as possible in the morning. I drained my glass, and his voice seemed once more to lilt and purr, conciliatory and oddly entrancing.

'How lucky for both of us that you're happy. We have something in common – our collaboration would have come to nought if you were ignorant of the happiness that's still feasible on this unhappy planet. Outsiders think husbands and wives who care for each other are bores. Society hostesses are not keen to entertain couples who keep on catching each other's eyes and hoping it's time to be alone together. Confirmed bachelors, involuntary spinsters and homosexuals have to be exceptionally generous to approve of Darby and Joan. Marriage is unfashionable, but we are writers and students of the history of literature, we know that good work is fated to be unfashionable, and therefore deduce that what is fashionable is usually bad, judging by high-class criteria. To spurn marriage, to denigrate it, to call it impossible, is to deny love – and that, in a word, is decadent. The bores are not those who have succeeded where many have failed. And decadence is not merely moral decline and the latest outrage of art, it's the death of culture and the end of humanity. We must talk more. We must put our heads together and save the world. But now I shall leave you, and return as soon as nature permits.'

He signalled somehow to Marie. She duly wheeled out an invalid chair that had also escaped my notice in the gloom. He transferred himself with the girl's help into the chair. Neither of them cast a glance in my direction as he was wheeled out of the room.

I was intrigued. Talk about what? He was a most unlikely saviour of the world, and I had no presumptuous aspirations in that line: what sort of salvation did he have in mind? And how could he spin high-falutin phrases in defence of matrimony five minutes after discussing Marie's musculature in the manner of an over-sexed adolescent?

I was bewildered as well as intrigued. He had been polite and rude to me, and teased and pleased or at least placated. All I was more or less sure of was that I felt like his plaything, to be shaken up and dusted down at his superior will.

I would leave in the morning. But I was disinclined to call a halt to the proceedings immediately. I drank some more wine and became conscious of a contrary excitement: what next, what surprises were in store for me? Everything was weird, not to say devilish – a wine that changed my mind, a host who subjected me to treatment reminiscent of the third degree, a hostess who presided from afar, a dreamlike villa behind gates that locked me in.

Time passed. I examined the wine bottles on the desk. The labels explained nothing. Through the library windows I could now see the lights of many other villas. And in the drawing-room when I wandered in there, the bay window showed a jewelled view of Villefranche, the looping street lamps on roads leading up to the *corniches*, the bright cafés along the waterfront, the headlights and red rear lights of occasional cars seeking room to park, and the illuminated caterpillar of a little train plying towards Nice from Monte Carlo.

Possibly I would be able to delay my departure for long enough to investigate that scene. Gerbert was unkind to have suggested that I could have brought Grace to the Villa Valerie. I wished in vain that she was with me and she and I could plumb the geographical and personal depths together. Villefranche must be within walking distance in one direction, just as St Jean Cap Ferrat and Beaulieu were in the other.

I re-established myself in my chair and waited in the darkened room until after seven o'clock.

He offered no apology. He did not ask for more light. Marie again sat at the desk, and the conversation to which she was not privy resumed.

'Have you read my books?' he asked.

'I read one long ago, and this afternoon I was again looking into your trilogy in my bedroom.'

'What's your verdict?'

'I'm not a critic.'

'You wouldn't be here if you were.'

'I don't have a verdict, but I'm envious of your style.'

'Faint praise!'

'Far from it! Style has wings, lack of style equals hobnailed boots. Besides, you broke new ground and made more money than most of us.'

He was silent. He stared at me or seemed to through his impenetrable glasses, and I was afraid I had upset him. Yet I drew the line at telling him lies about his work.

Inconsequentially he asked: 'Did you ever win a scholarship? Did you ever have to?'

'No.'

'Of course, you're upper class.'

I repudiated the charge, although he seemed not to be sneering at me: 'I cut my class links fifty years ago.'

Again disconnectedly he remarked: 'The trilogy's as terrible as they said it was.'

'Prudes and prigs tacked that epithet on to it,' I commented with consoling intentions.

'They were right. I agree with them. I'm ashamed of my books. I'd burn all the books I've written if I could. I'm woken at night by regrets.'

He could not have surprised me more. Where was his arrogance? He might look proud, but the words he articulated beautifully were abject.

I cleared my throat preparatory to doling out comfort, but he interrupted.

'Your boast is that you're not a toff, mine would be that I am. Opposites connect up somewhere, don't they? Here we are in the same boat! Your birth and breeding wasn't your fault any more than mine was. But I was too clever for my own good, and always under pressure to be top of the class. When I had no more classes to be top of, when I was sick of being nobody,

I wrote *Defecation*. It was easy. The subject wasn't hard to find. I simply looked down the list of taboos, and I was rich overnight. The public has always had vicious tastes, and always pays for what is worse than the thing before. The book may be defensible, it describes experience common to all God's children, and hypocrites would say its justification is that it supplies the demand of the people – but I hate it. I burn with shame to think of my other books that cashed in on the first one. Please don't argue, I have no time to argue!'

After a moment's thought he resumed: 'The relationship between money and art is the last best story in the world. There's no art without money, and not much with it. To start with I was too poor to write a good book, then I was too rich. I worked for money's sake. I became a literary prostitute, and when I had enough money I bought position, status, power and the other stuff you say you chucked overboard. What a game, society's game of snakes and ladders! What a stupid story! You probably know the rest. I retired, stopped writing, I'd run through a few fortunes, and I shook the sand or the dirt of my native land from my feet. Ungratefully I no longer loved the country that had done me favours, I loathed its ignorance, I detested its journalists, although they may be necessary evils. I was at a very low ebb when I met my wife.'

He began to cough. Marie arose and stepping round the desk bent over him. But he waved her away and she returned with impassive face and bowed head to her chair.

'You must call me Gerbert. The sir is an excrescence – Gerbert has connections with an authority greater than some civil servant in Whitehall.'

Was he joking? The light of the lamp shone across his face, etching deep shadows. Yet his expression, so far as I could see, was neither humorous nor hellish.

He carried on: 'I'm not proud of my writings. Am I the only author in the world who isn't proud of any of his publications? My vanity is reserved for an achievement of a different sort. At a late age, when men lose their manhood and their memories, when I was under no pressure to do anything except die, I performed a rare feat although I say so myself. I was receptive to inspiration and changed my mind, ideas, beliefs, my persona, my self. I'm not speaking of development, I mean transformation. The hope that people will change for the better, that the fibre of their beings will improve out of recognition, is the commonest of all the illusions. I have nothing to show for my feeling of being the exception that proves the rule. And I lack the strength to plan, organise, transcribe or stick to the long-drawn-out business of another book. There's the rub! I have reason to believe that my mistakes are rectified and redeemed, and that the experience and the implications of my redemption might be of use and value to others. I'm convinced that at last I have something worthwhile to say, and I'm as it were dumb. Are you going to help me?'

Before I could answer, Lee opened the library door. His toothy smiles and outlandish utterances announced dinner.

I ate by myself again. I was ushered out of the library, Gerbert did not follow, and in the dining-room Mrs Lee pointed to the solitary place laid on the table and the chair I had occupied at lunchtime. I did not object. A pause for reflection, a break from being stared and talked at, were welcome; but so would have been a polite gesture and an excusatory word. No doubt he needed to rest, to have special food, eat without interruption and prepare for our next session.

Dinner was as delicious as lunch – fish soup, steak and the sort of chips called *allumettes* or matchsticks and baked chicory, local soft cheese, more red wine and then coffee. Mrs Lee waddled in and out with it, smiling a lot although with fewer teeth than her husband, rattling instructions – probably 'Eat it all up!' and 'Why haven't you eaten more?' – and fixing me with her darting wary eyes. Lee must have been attending to his boss. At the end of my meal, after an hour or thereabouts, he entered the dining-room and Mrs Lee helped or half-pulled me out of my chair and pointed in the direction of the library – her signal for describing what was in store consisted of snapping her fingers and thumb together near her mouth to indicate jaw-jaw.

The scene was exactly the same – Gerbert sitting there like some old guru or witch doctor with the girl in white; the pool of light amongst the shadows; the dark adjoining room; and the almost deathly silence contrasting with the views through the windows of the jolly illuminations of Villefranche.

I returned to my place in the *tableau vivant*, and Gerbert inquired: 'Well?'

I did not understand him.

He began again: 'I beg your pardon. I have forgotten my manners, amongst other things. Regrettably, food has become more pain than pleasure for my antiquated digestion, and I prefer not to share the ordeal with my guests. I should have explained, I'm sorry. I trust that my table, as your father might have referred to the meat and drink in question, or the victuals on offer, as my father would have said, have been to your liking?'

I replied affirmatively.

'And the arrangements upstairs?'

I repeated myself.

'I've read none of your books,' he said, 'but I gather they've been applauded by the press.'

It occurred to me to thank him, but I stopped myself – was he praising or disparaging me? – and struck a cautious note: 'I retired some months ago.'

'Ah yes!' He sounded incredulous. 'I retired too.'

'We moved house and I intend to do no more writing,' I insisted.

'Does your wife believe that?'

He had caught me out, and I laughed and admitted: 'Not necessarily.'

He observed: 'If Shakespeare really did retire to Stratford-on-Avon, Bacon must have written his plays. The habit of literary work is unbreakable in my experience. Scribes and storytellers continue to write in their heads long after they have ceased to be able to put pen to paper.'

'Maybe – but that's a generalisation – the truth's supposed to reside in the particular case, for instance mine.'

'Why did you come here if you're in retirement?'

He had caught me again, caught me napping at least, and my answer was wriggly: 'I came for the ride, because you were generous enough to send me a ticket and money to get me home, and I felt obliged to hear what it was all about.'

'Well?' he queried again. 'Are you going to help?'

'Help how? What would be the subject of this book you have in mind? Would it be autobiographical?'

He began to cough. As before, Marie approached in order to render assistance. She therefore interposed herself between him and me, but not until I had observed that instead of waving her away he raised his reddened face with ballooning cheeks to hers in a rather imploring fashion. He coughed retchingly, and I feared for a moment that he might expire. But some traffic took place – Marie delved and fumbled in the pockets of her overall – his throat was sprayed or a pill given – and he desisted. She wiped his brow with a cloth or tissue, and went back to her chair without looking at me.

His recovery was complete. He had recovered his composure, and his voice had not lost its silkinesss. He said in a dismissive tone, 'Excuse me,' referring to his coughing fit, and then answered my questions.

'Authors should not discuss their books in the making, nor their books that are made. But present circumstances are exceptional, as I have told you. My mind and my heart are full of an account of love in the abstract, love from its lowest base to its highest achievement in principle more than in practice. Physical love is finite – I exhausted that subject, and was mistaken to hope that I was giving my readers a lesson to live by. Sex is fine but fleeting, safe sex ringed round with qualifications and reservations and caution and scepticism is nice while it lasts, but love is another word and something else. I would analyse the progression of love from nadir to zenith, and not autobiographically, not egoistically, as you might suspect. I am asking you for six evenings of attendance to the summing-up of a long life's study of Venus in all her manifestations.'

I replied readily: 'I'm afraid it's too late for me to become a ghost – or should I say too early?'

He ignored my refusal, my pleasantry, and continued: 'The

fee of ten thousand pounds is conditional upon an agreement between gentlemen, although you say you have chosen not to be a gentleman and in fact I never was one – no contracts will be signed. I trust you will consider the offer as set out in my solicitor's letter is binding, as I do. My ideas, my communications, will be a gift for you to revise, express, use, sell or publish however you think fit. I require, I only insist upon, no credit, dedication, honour, glory, payment or recompense – I hereby become anonymous. You would be the sole author of any book that happened to be the harvest of the six more evenings I beg you to spend with me.'

He had again surprised me by the absence of strings attached, but I managed to say: 'I'm flattered, and I'm sure I would be fascinated, even if I don't quite understand the whys and wherefores. The point is – my point – that I really have decided not to take on such a commitment or any more literary work.'

'You must not be hasty. I respect your integrity as well as your talent, and can be patient. Six evenings, three or four hours multiplied by six, are a lot of time for a man of my age but not for a man of yours; and I suggest that your vocation would be pleased to have a project and your existence would benefit from my bounty in the otherwise empty and possibly expensive years stretching ahead of you.'

'I'm sorry.'

I did not altogether like his tone and determined not to surrender.

He signed to Marie and addressed me: 'Please excuse me for leaving you. I have to harbour my strength or hide my weakness. I still retire early in the vain hope of being capable of clear-headed composition in the morning, and maybe I shall be glad to have done so when tomorrow evening comes. Anyway, before I abandon you to the mind-blowing pleasures of my house and garden, please join me in a toast to our old profession and our new acquaintanceship.'

I did not want to, I had resolved not to drink another drop of his dangerous wine; but Marie again knelt before me, I felt it would be wrong also to turn down this latest offer, and I took the glass and duly drank the contents.

'Incidentally,' he remarked, 'I assume you know the origins of my name and the powers attributed to the first and the second holders of it?'

He was already being wheeled towards the door. I answered his question, I may even have mentioned Faust, then pursued him hurriedly to say I would be leaving in the morning and to thank and bid him goodbye. But I was too late.

In the doorway he intoned over his shoulder, '*Au revoir*,' and for some reason I left it at that.

The Lower Depths

The next morning I walked into the village of St Jean Cap Ferrat and at ten o'clock made the telephone call that Grace received – thanks to the hour's difference between French and English time – at nine.

'My darling,' I began.

'I'm missing you,' she returned.

'Same here.'

'Crystal's missing you too. She waits and watches by the front door.'

'I'll soon be home.'

'Today, you mean?'

'That depends. Are you all right?'

'Yes. Are you?'

'More or less.'

'Why? What's happened?'

'Nothing's happened. How's Oliver?'

'Oliver's Oliver. What's it like? Tell me.'

'Astonishing – more so than I thought it was yesterday – I spent the evening with Gerbert.'

'Is he Faust all over again?'

'I don't know.'

'I was joking. Are you serious?'

I described his appearance, dark glasses and beard, immobility, enigmatic conversation, alluring speaking voice, and the library, the single lamp shining in my eyes, the girl who knelt and nursed him, and the wine and what might be called his parting shot.

'He said *"au revoir"* although he knew you were leaving this morning and wouldn't be seeing him again?'

'Not exactly. I'd made it clear that I refused his offer. He should have known that I wouldn't stay on in his house.'

'Didn't you say goodbye?'

'I tried to. But he was being wheeled out of the room. He called *"au revoir"* over his shoulder and I didn't argue the point.'

'How much of his wine had you drunk?'

'I wasn't tipsy. I admit I was a bit bewildered by the peculiarity of everything.'

'What sort of wine was it? You don't usually lift your elbow.'

'Good wine, delicious wine, of which I probably should have partaken with the aid of a long spoon.'

'Are you joking now?'

'All I know is that every time I drank some I found myself in agreement with him or almost.'

'Do you mean he's in league with the devil?'

'He wouldn't mind me thinking he was.'

'Do you want to see him again?'

'Not much.'

'A little?'

'I'd be embarrassed to invade his privacy to say goodbye, and I doubt I'd get an airline ticket for today at such short notice.'

'Could you stay at the Villa for an extra night without involving yourself in his plots and plans?'

'Hardly – he only needs me for six nights in all – that's the deal – I am or I was an employee on approval, not a guest.'

'Has he been nice to you?'

'Oh yes – and persuasive and insidious. We do have our profession in common, we're two old novelists playing a game of cards with aces up our sleeves – it's quite amusing. He makes out that writing's a chronic constitutional defect and that I'll be done for without work in progress – work for him, that's to say.'

'But he's retired and written nothing for years.'

'Exactly – for twenty-odd years.'

'Did you agree with him?'

'No.'

'I'm not keen to be one of those wives who stop their husbands writing.'

'You've never stopped me, you never would – on the contrary.'

'What does his employment boil down to?'

'Money for jam! He'll give me ideas which I'm at liberty to convert or not to convert into a book. He seems to want to air his views and doesn't care whether or not they ever see the light of day. The bottom line is that he'll pay me ten thousand pounds for listening to him for a few hours for one day less than a week.'

'What's the catch?'

'None that I can detect so far.'

'What ideas do you expect they'll be?'

'His ideas of love.'

'Good gracious, you'd be covered in smut by the end of the six sessions!'

'He says he's reformed his character, in fact transformed himself, and he's ashamed of all his books and has learned lessons of universal significance.'

'Do you believe that?'

'He's hoping I'll correct the impression he spread about that sex is the solution to the problem of life.'

'But love's such an old story, it's been told so often!'

'Perhaps he knows something we don't know – his wife's French after all.'

'Can you trust him? Can you be sure he wouldn't sue you for plagiarism after the work was done?'

'I can't yet – I might be surer if I'd spent more time in his company.'

'Why don't you?'

'Because we're missing each other.'

'But Oliver's here, and I don't want him to exasperate both of us.'

'Would we survive a whole week apart?'

'Shouldn't we be mercenary for a change?'

The last two questions settled the matter, and the rest of our conversation was private.

I was in a cafe called *L'Elisir* in the open space – in no sense a square – overlooking the marina in St Jean Cap Ferrat. The proprietor spoke English – *un peu* – and had allowed me to use his telephone – I had not had to put coins in slots, and could perch on a stool at the bar instead of standing and sweating in a public phone box. When I reluctantly rang off, I ordered tea with lemon and went and sat out of doors at one of the tables in the morning sunshine.

I had been the only customer in the bar except for a pensioner who popped in for an unhealthy breakfast of coffee and brandy, and no one else was sitting out. The proprietor or barman was thirtyish, dark and smart with his shirtsleeves rolled up above his elbows, and talked to me for a minute after bringing my tea and a bill that included the telephone call. He cracked an example of the laboured jokes that foreigners are so inclined to attempt in our difficult language.

'I ham John of Saint John,' he said. *'Je m'appelle Jean.'*

I also introduced myself and we shook hands.

'You are ear for *tourisme*?' he inquired.

For business and pleasure, I replied, at which he rubbed an index finger and thumb together in the international dumbshow for money-grubbing.

I changed the subject and remarked at the loveliness of the weather, which elicited his dismissive comment: 'Is winter.' Two ladies in fur coats plus a tiny shivering poodle sat down at a nearby table and seemed to prove his point. When I insisted that the weather was lovely whatever the season, he said with a Gallic shrug, 'Is normal,' and translated unnecessarily, *'C'est normal.'*

I stirred lemon and sugar into my tea. I had time to burn: at the Villa Valerie while eating my breakfast of warm buttery croissants and fresh crisp rolls and butter and apricot jam, I had somehow made it clear to the Indonesians that I would soon leave the house and return round about four.

Cap means headland in French, a tongue of land protruding into the sea, and from my seat in St Jean I looked back at the coastline of Beaulieu and Roquebrune under the great green foothills of the Alpes Maritimes, and possibly Monte Carlo in the hazy distance. In due course I wandered down to the marina and, inspecting the serried ranks of luxurious yachts, thanked God for capitalism which provides us all with the unending interest of the spectacle of wealth. Then I took directions from an amiable passer-by and walked uphill and out of the village and by a circuitous route to the Villa Ephrussi de Rothschild, which stands on the crest of the ridge.

I had read about this sight to be seen and local landmark in guide books. A Rothschild heiress married to Maurice Ephrussi built and furnished the house in the early years of the century. Full-scale models were constructed before she gave the go-ahead to her architects and builders. Then her agents combed the world for antiques and artefacts, and rumour relates that she chose the stuff she wanted on the platform of Beaulieu station. But she only lived there for a few months and after her death the place was presented to the French nation.

The site is magnificent, as are the views both east and west, also out to sea and north at the mountains. The house looks down on St Jean on one side and Villefranche on the other, and is a grand and glorious pink and white fantasy. It has pillars and porches, at least one oriel window, plasterwork and Grecian friezes, an eccentric afterthought or two in bricks and mortar, a fine regular south-facing facade, and altogether corroborates the truth yet again that architecture – and perhaps art – is most successful when subject to the control of enlightened patronage. The interior is a series of rooms leading off a square hall or atrium reaching to the roof: those on the ground floor are full of treasures but not excessively large, and would be filled with light if blinds were not drawn to protect tapestries and rugs, painted furniture and inlaid wood floors. The gardens are French, English, Spanish and so on, and more geographical than pretty.

I spent the middle of the day in this peaceful ambience under the cerulean sky and in the warming sunshine. Nobody forced me to do anything against my will. I had a snack to eat in the restaurant operating in Madame Ephrussi's ballroom and relaxed on her elaborate garden seats, and strolled back to base via different roads, some of which bordered romantic inlets of completely clear water shaded by cliffs and pines.

I had been dreading my return and trying not to think Grace and I had made a mistake. Would Gerbert with his Faustian affectations allow me to escape in six days? But, when I reached the gates of the estate and waited for the Indonesians to admit me, the spell of the baobab, of the long lawn under the rare trees, of the veiled aspect of the house and prevailing quietude, reasserted itself. I walked in more gladly than I had thought I would, and saw through the mistiness, or the steam rising from the watered greenery, cars and figures on the gravel circle.

The two cars were French, an old Citroën *deux chevaux* with scars and soft top, and a Citroën limousine, looking new and sleek. Strangers were emerging from the front door, a box-shaped middle-aged woman accompanied by Marie who carried electrical contraptions, and, followed by Lee and Mrs Lee, a hairy man in a charcoal grey flannel suit bearing a fat briefcase. Predictably, the latter approached the more luxurious car; unpredictably, he was talking to the Indonesians in their language.

He shook my hand in the French fashion and said in reasonable English that he was Kolnatsch, the Aucotts' solicitor based in Nice, and that he came to the Villa Valerie on most days to render additional assistance as interpreter. He spelt his name for my benefit: why do so many French people have foreign names? He had a black beard and thick bouncy black hair, seemed to know who I was and what I was doing, introduced me to 'Sir Aucott's' physiotherapist, and drove off too fast, kicking up gravel with his car's wheels. The physio with her infra-red lamp on the passenger seat of her 'two-horse' vehicle drummed and thundered in pursuit.

Mrs Lee smiled at me, nearly closing her eyes; Lee showed amusement at having to push the gravel back into position with his bare hands; and I was quite impatient to listen and with luck learn something in the library in a couple of hours.

*

'We must never forget,' he said in his mellifluous voice, 'we must all remember that we may be no more than lichen on the face of one of the numberless astral bodies floating about in an illimitable universe. Our palaces, relatively speaking, could be smaller than particles of dust. What importance can therefore be attached to our passions and our cares? Judging by size, we're the next best thing to ciphers and noughts.

'Yet lichens are not without ambition. They are prepared to fight to survive. They have their appetites and can reproduce themselves. A similar description would fit our brothers and sisters who form a majority of mankind.

'Don't expect me to mince matters at my time of life. I shocked people once before for what I now consider the wrong reason; for reasons I believe are right I'm again ready to shock – and I'm too old and rich to fear the prejudices of liberals. Here's a heresy for you: all men are not born equal. Here's another: human rights do not exist – nobody has a right to anything. And lust and greed are what make the wider world go round. And intelligence, idealism, talent and truth are reserved for the happy few.

'We evolved from apes, according to the latest guess of pundits, who arrive at their conclusions by means of errors. Chimps do exhibit some of the characteristics of the human race, for instance sensationalism and cruelty for cruelty's sake. Female naturalists are apt to think chimps are so like human beings that they foster and adopt them; and maybe such women are not far wrong inasmuch as they are usually attacked by their charges.

'Science, unlike journalism, does not get everything wrong. We owe it a debt of gratitude for its peaceable inventions. However, if God is meant to have integrity, if the gods are meant to be trustworthy, we should not bow down before science and worship it. All too human are its contrariness and inconsistency. It would save life with one hand and destroy life with the other. It has begun to make babies by taking advantage of nature even as, with the complicity of politicians, it kills babies.

'Abortion isn't an issue that should be tackled by a man who derived the major pleasures of his existence from the opposite sex. My personality is or was impulsive, and many of the women whose favours I pleaded for were obliging and reckless. Not only should I refrain from biting hands that were ready to cover up the misdemeanours of passion and ignorance in those days, but as an ex-novelist I should know better than to enter the political lists, where the fate of children in the womb is now squabbled over by self-styled adults.

'Politics are ephemeral, and to base fiction on today's political controversy is more than likely to be out of date tomorrow. But now I am talking, not writing, and referring to eternal verities, no longer spinning yarns. Furthermore, I am almost beyond the reach of politicians and not scared by their power and their tendencies to do damage.

'My objection to abortion on demand is objective, no longer influenced by my sympathy for generous girls who get into trouble, ethical judged by the criteria of history, and above all practical. The lawful licence to terminate pregnancies creates more problems that it solves, or, rather, destroys more than healthy children in the womb. Politics and science in unholy alliance, by getting round the rules of nature, by not respecting the condition that nature applies to sex, put licentiousness before love, trivialise and mock the solemnity of love, and knock the ultimate nail into love's coffin – and without love what's left of the human spirit, of humanity, how are we to cooperate and live at peace, what do we have to be proud of, what can we hope for, what will become of us?

'I have not contracted the commonest geriatric disease, paranoia. I am not making a mountain out of a molehill. Forgive me for reminding you that your suspicions and scepticism are out of order in this century. The work of an obscure German Jewish refugee, who spent his days in the British Museum and read Dickens to his children in the evenings, scarcely amounted to a molehill; yet from 1917 until today it has accounted for billions of deaths and casualties and has not yet finished killing. The seeds of great disasters may not amount to much. You cannot accuse me of exaggeration if you recall the history of Marxism, of Karl Marx's hateful little tract, which already accounts for nearly a hundred years of savagery without parallel.

'The love of a mother for her child sets a standard and creates a precedent. It's the least selfish form of loving, and the closest to the message of Christianity. Of course love's as individualistic as we are, and not necessarily reproductive; but everyone has been dependent upon the love of a mother and her readiness to suffer in order to bring us into the world.

'And sooner or later almost everyone seeks to commune with somebody else. But the consummation of that search, of romance or lust, without payment, penalty, obligation, responsibility, without control or care, without recognition of the natural purpose and consequences of the act, deals love the most grievous of blows. Acceptance of the possibility or the likelihood that copulation will be the cause of cold-blooded murder not only undermines morality, it's bound to provoke nature, perhaps has started to provoke it, to hit back.

'I seem to see that the keystone of the arch of love has been stolen, and the stone upon stone supporting it, all the relationships that dignified our existence and expressed our better intentions, are falling down and being scattered far and wide.

'I was one of the vandals. I put fornication first. Women tempted me to do it: but just as Eve made amends for her mistake in the garden of Eden by providing Adam with the services that populated the world, so a daughter of Eve and the dearest of women has inspired me to atone for my sin by bequeathing my experience of loving and hating to those who are neither selfish nor homicidal and would wish humanity to survive.'

Dinner was announced.

I hope the above does justice to Gerbert, although I cannot reproduce the fluent and irrecoverable sweetness of his delivery. I have racked my memory for what he said, and paraphrased and abbreviated, and done my best. Whether or not I agree with him or approve is beside the point: at the time I was impressed by his argument and swept along by his eloquence, and now I would be sorry to fail him.

I adjourned to the dining-room as on the previous evening, and ate another excellent meal and partook more cautiously of the wine. I was afraid of forgetting, even if my intention was still to depart in the morning and not to undertake the commission. When I heard the wheelchair being trundled back to the library, I drank a quick extra cup of coffee which might be an aid to concentration.

'Have you read *The Symposium* recently?'

The question was rhetorical, for he continued without waiting for my answer. The scene was the same: that stony countenance, theatrically lit, confronted me, while Marie sat still as a statue yet alert to the needs of our employer.

'For a negative reason the book merits a glance, because of the relief of not finding oneself at the dinner party Plato describes. All-male all-night gatherings, with intellectual back-chat and long-winded speeches and most guests pie-eyed at the end, never were my idea of fun. The discussion of love would be more worthwhile if Socrates was not such a bully and his interrogations were not so cerebral; and its seriousness would be more useful if the love discussed was not exclusively between men.

'Plato's vision of the differing degrees and qualities of love, of the class system of love, has some validity. Yet that Athenian dinner is actually and mainly understandable by and of interest to antiquarians. I would not presume to emulate Plato; on the contrary I pay him the compliment of asserting that for a modern readership his dissertation has to be renewed and given the heterosexual dimension. The theory that high love is only possible between one man and another was superseded not long after he advanced it – nature was kind enough to our species to make sure that it didn't catch on.

'Homosexuality today is fashionable and does not pretend to be platonic. No doubt the male version can boast examples of complete and true love, while lesbianism is noted for its capability of selfless devotion. The fact remains that these orientations are barren, dead ends in a procreative sense, therefore without nature's blessing, and not part of my own reflections on the emotions to which I owe my being.

'Besides, I will not break the first and last rule of literary tact and expatiate on a subject beyond my experience.

'An equivalent objection applies to heterosexual relations of the most basic kind. I know nothing of coupling in ditches, of minutes of madness in a dark doorway, and won't compound my offences by reproducing – regurgitating – those sexual fantasies that made my name and are lining the pockets and especially the purses of other writers. Besides, a record of the realities of low life and low love is now kept by films and television rather than by words written by types who are supposed to be educated – cameras are more prurient than authors.

'However, one case of love on the wild side – which I understand is the up-to-date euphemism descriptive of sordid entanglements – forms the first step of my staircase to the stars. It was brought to my attention by two letters – I still receive fan mail, I regret to say, pleas for advice from misguided souls who regard me as an expert in the fields of excretion, onanism and fornication. This correspondent was male, lower-middle-class, I guess, and spared me no detail of the intimate secrets of his marriage. I shall call him John and misname his wife Felicity, and the novelist in me will probably add a little local colour to his account of his problems.

'John met Felicity when he was twenty-five and she was nineteen, and courted her for four years. He worked in a bank, she was the only child of divorced parents and was reared by a doting mother – her father remarried and steered clear of his first family. Felicity was neurotic, suffered from eating disorders, was whimsical and spoilt, and considered herself John's social superior; but she was pretty, as intriguing as only neurosis can be, and he thought she was perfect and wanted to marry her. The courtship seems to have been scarred by her hesitations, tantrums, retreats and elusiveness, but he stuck it out, a single sexual exchange of a muddled sort took place, they became engaged and tied the knot.

'Her virginity caused pain and unpleasantness on the honeymoon. But he was determined to make up for lost time and excited by having to claim his marital right, and she submitted with sulky passivity. At home they were not comfortable, let alone happy. She was an inefficient housewife, a spendthrift and hypochondriac, subject to crazes for disgusting diets and cultish religion. He often had to cook his own supper, and was increasingly depressed by her demands for money and her patronising attitude to his relations and his work. But she still had the power to charm and attract him with her dainty ways and sudden shows of kittenish affection.

'They rubbed along for a year or two. Then she got hold of a book on feminism. Perhaps it was a mischievous book, perhaps she misunderstood the feminist message. Anyway she was instantly converted to the belief that her behaviour was not loveless and selfish, but the stirrings of her participation in the crusade of women against the tyranny of men. She now refused to do housework on principle. She was not sorry to cause John financial headaches. She quarrelled with her old-fashioned father-in-law and despised her mother-in-law for being contented with her lot as well as common. She decided that the conduct of her own errant father was typical. But sex became her battleground.

'Felicity was like many women, even women in the sex-mad present, I suspect, and certainly like the majority of men: she was ignorant of the mechanics of the genital equipment of her opposite number, and not much more knowledgeable about her own. She had no brothers, her mother was prudish, and she had never seen John in the altogether – their love was made in the dark, she had always stipulated it, and had locked their bathroom door against him. She kept her hands to herself during sexual action and, because she said she was not ready to bear his child, insisted on his wearing a strong condom.

'Her brand of feminism gave her confidence. She deduced that she had been raped by her husband, repeatedly raped, and that it was high time to get her own back. Her objections to John turned into anger, vengeful wrath justified by millions of years of the persecution of women by men. She would therefore wait for him to return from a long day at the bank in the sitting-room of their home with the curtains drawn and no clothes on. When he said and proved that he was tired, she accused him of not loving her, of wasting his substance on a mistress, of deliberately humiliating her and not keeping his side of the sexual bargain.

'Since she was determined to live as freely as men did, and without the ball and chain of motherhood, she made things more difficult for John by cross-questioning him about the tight fit of his condom and by filling herself to the brim with spermicidal foam. His failures annoyed her as much as his successes had done. She would not accept his explanations and excuses, was convinced he disappointed her on purpose, and guaranteed more failures by threatening to sue for her legal share of the fun he had had.

'The rude vernacular applies the epithet "stupid" to the female organ with reason, because it has no power of discrimination or very little, and no in-built defences. Felicity imagined she could force John as she felt she had been forced, and that her off-putting foreplay would make no more difference to his faculty than his disregard of her wishes had made to hers. She thought a woman could rape a man as easily as vice versa, and that his lack of cooperation was further evidence of the conspiracy of the stronger sex to persecute the weaker.

'Deep discussion of the problem was out of the question. Running commentaries on sexual communing are rare the world over, because partners are applying themselves separately to the effort of consummation, because the physiological process is impossible to describe except by doctors, because moans and groans are the best defence against a sense of the ridiculous spoiling the sport, and because shyness and fastidiousness are not exclusively Anglo-Saxon defects or qualities.

'Characteristically and contrarily, although Felicity had not enjoyed her husband's attentions while they were forthcoming, she found that her flesh had acquired a taste for them and was almost addicted. She not only wanted to superimpose her will on his, she wanted satisfaction, and the two wants combined to reinforce her emotional and physical assaults on his person. Their resentment became mutual, and their quarrels deteriorated into talk of divorce. At last she hurled the question at him, "Will you ever?" – and he could supply this demand of hers at least to the extent of answering "Never!" – and they passed the point of no return.'

'It was some months after their divorce that John wrote his first letter to me, describing the *via dolorosa* of the marriage,' Gerbert resumed after a break. 'He was licking his wounds in a lodging house and can't have had much to do in the evenings. I refrained from replying – I've never suffered fools gladly, and was not prepared to waste my time and add insult to his injuries by telling him home truths.

'But years elapsed, possibly a dozen years, and I received a second letter which reminded me of the first and carried the tragical comedy a stage further.

'John did not hold my unresponsiveness against me – he was a masochist. He seemed to need to make a clean breast of his difficulties, and had settled on me as the recipient of his tale of woe. He had not done badly in a worldly sense, he had a better job at the bank, a house of his own, savings and a pension. But his private life was empty and lonely, and he was now impaled upon the horns of a dilemma.

'Chastity had been his lot since he last wrote. The one lesson he had apparently learned from his marriage was that he could not function under pressure. He realised that he required affection and encouragement in order to do his trick, and Felicity had broken his nerve so far as trying again matrimonially. His search for consolation in extra-marital arms had also ended in fiasco: he put it graphically by confessing that he died below the belt in company, and that manual and other shots at resuscitation made him feel like a corpse in the keeping of a necrophiliac.

'That he was unwilling to risk another repetition of the shame of his impotence was by no means the worst bit of his bad news. Felicity had kept in telephonic and postal touch with him. Intermittently she communicated in order to demand money and to taunt him. Her taunts were designed not only to punish him for having been unappreciative of her charms, but also to prove she was capable of attracting better stronger men than her ex-husband. Her motivation and her conversation were almost equally objectionable: she talked in the way that her brand of feminism imagined was unisex, that is more manly than womanly. She boasted of her promiscuity in obscene terms – one night stands, rough trade, men she compared to seaside donkeys, multiple orgasms. Sometimes she sent him upsetting photographs of herself, topless at a rave, for instance, and unsuitably dressed in tight T-shirt, hot pants and hobnailed boots sitting on the lap of a brute of a man who looked like the missing link.

'Her sexual beano was brought to an end by the birth of a baby, her son, called Teddy after the bear. Teddy was a bastard in every sense – his father was either not known or never named – Felicity would rather die than share him with a man. She doted on and spoilt the child, and said she was happy at last. And John was prepared to pay her even more money to keep her quiet or quieter.

'But why he had picked up his pen again was that he had just seen her, and she had asked him to remarry her or at least protect her. Teddy, whom John had not been allowed to meet, had grown into a big boy for his eleven years, was nearly six foot tall and weighed eleven stone, and was a misfit and malcontent imbued with adolescent hatred and violent inclinations. He had taken to striking his mother. He was the agent of her broken nose, black eye, arm in plaster and sundry bruises. The story she sobbed on John's shoulder was that she had never been able to control her Teddy, who owed his existence to some sperm she had bought on the continent no doubt provided by a psychopath. Yes, she had impregnated herself with a turkey-baster, and as a result was in fear and trembling.

'Should he or should he not take pity on her? That was John's dilemma and question.

'I was roused to answer this time round. So-called poetic justice, although there was not much poetry in the situation, had caught up with the pair of them, I wrote back. Felicity was not one of the avenging angels of female subjugation throughout history, as she was pleased to think she was, but a blameworthy wife, the exact opposite of a helpmeet, a half-baked nympho and an irresponsible mother. She presumed she knew better than nature, religion, tradition and available experience, had conducted herself cruelly and disgustingly, and deserved to be murdered in the bed she had made and would have to lie on. Above all, far from doing the sisters of her sex a favour, she had helped to rob them of the respect that was their shield against the importunities of men.

'As for John himself, he was not much better than she was, since he had chosen to court and marry her just as she had chosen to say yes. They had embraced their fate; and foolishness was no excuse, and ignorance a feeble one. He had let himself be castrated by a wife who had let him overrule her signals that she did not want to marry him. The consequence was misery, and trouble in store for all concerned, probably in future including the police and social services – and in my opinion, an opinion in these topsy-turvy days more than likely to be considered outrageous and unhelpful, it was their own fault.

'No, I threw John no lifeline – too many undeserving people are saved, now everybody's saving somebody else or some building or animal or insect or weed. His dilemma was his business, not mine, and I had no confidence in his ability or in hers to stop making mistakes. Moreover, I guessed he communicated merely to complain and for consolation, and the latter I was unwilling to dish out. He and his Felicity were not criminals; nor were they exactly denizens of the lower depths of human intercourse. He was outwardly respectable and decent, and so far as I know she steered clear of abortionists. But he despite his respectability and she despite her social superiority had sunk and were sinking into the mire, and they were a disgrace to love.'

Natural Selection

It was the next morning, and I was back in St Jean later than intended, at eleven or so, at *L'Elisir* or John's of St John, speaking to Grace on the telephone.

'I was starting to worry,' she said.

My apology for being late included the explanation that I had been jotting down all I could remember of Gerbert's discourse or diatribe.

'What was it like?' she asked.

Extraordinary, I replied, a hell-fire sermon, a verbal tract for the times, a modern morality, a marathon for a man of his age at any rate – getting on for three hours of nonstop chinwag delivered with no notes, hardly a hesitation, and perfect lucidity in his mesmeric voice, which reminded me of the sirens' songs that lured mariners on to the rocks.'

'What did he have to say?'

'A lot – and a lot I've forgotten. For one thing he's against abortion on demand. He thinks it's bad for love and the beginning of the end for all of us.'

'Don't other people think it's good for love, for free love anyway?'

'He's against free love too. He's like one of those converts who believe in everything they disbelieved before they were on their deathbeds. He harps on the discipline of love, and nature's penalties for breaking its laws. He's all for nature, and he ended by telling a cautionary tale about a feminist who overlooked the fact that men and woman are made differently in the vital area.'

'The feminist was in for a surprise.'

I laughed and explained further: 'Nature wreaks revenge, and Gerbert puts his boot in, because the feminist tries to have her cake and eat it – to behave like both sexes at the same time – and because her husband has no sense of self-preservation.'

'Was it interesting?'

'Impressive – but whether or not I could ever write an acceptable recap of so much controversial verbiage is a moot point. Gerbert's beyond me, I don't begin to understand him. He sits in his dimly lit library in the night, staring at me through sun-glasses and ignoring me – he could well be the devil's puppet if he didn't presume to lay down the law for almighty nature and love.'

'He sounds frightful.'

'Frightening maybe, but clever, original, rather admirable, and mysterious. Why didn't he tape-record his stuff? I'd like to ask him the question that debutantes ask their first boyfriends: why me? He's pretty frightful with his servants. He can't speak their language any more than I can.'

'Doesn't he try?'

'Not in my hearing – communication is by signs and third parties. He said he's glad not to have to waste his time gossiping with domestics.'

'Oh dear! How do you manage to communicate with them?'

'Likewise – but I hope my signs are more friendly than his. And now I've met his French solicitor as well as his Welsh one – Monsieur Kolnatsch, who can speak Indonesian and clocks in at the Villa Valerie to interpret and issue orders. Monsieur Kolnatsch works in Nice – where he springs from is another mystery – he's the blackest white man imaginable – but he's polite to me. What a set-up I've found myself in the middle of!'

'You won't get into trouble, will you?'

'No.'

'And you won't drink too much of that wine?'

'No.'

'Are you going to see the week out?'

'Well . . .'

John was indicating that he required his telephone, and at

the same time Grace told me that Oliver wanted her to fetch or carry something else for him.

How was she, I asked. Did she promise she was not allowing Oliver to exhaust her? Would she mind if I listened to Gerbert for one more night? Could she answer quickly as I would have to ring off in a minute?

She was fine, she replied, and Oliver was just about under control, and Crystal was her comfort and joy although the poor dog spent hours waiting for me, and I was not to think of returning until I was ready to – now there were only five more days to go before I was back at home and we could all live happily ever after.

We rang off, and at John's instigation I then walked from St Jean to Beaulieu by a coastal road designed more for pedestrians than cars. It was by the edge of the clean clear sea, which above rocks was the brown of English trout streams, and the purest aquamarine over a sandy bottom; and it faced eastwards and was bathed in sunlight.

Expensive villas reared up on the other side of the walkway, or crouched under pines, or were hidden from prying eyes by high walls and electronic gates. French dogs were walked here in the mornings, often by mistresses wearing fur coats even in this sort of weather, or by masters of a certain age smartly attired in Burberrys and soft Italian footwear. The dogs were mostly poodles and fox terriers: the latter brought to mind the headline I had seen in a newspaper displayed outside a newsagent's in St Jean, '*Toute la France aime le Fox*'. They – the dogs – looked in the pink of condition and as if they too enjoyed French cooking.

Beaulieu on my right had a neat little beach backed by gardens and overseen by an ugly angular building. I recognised it from the picture in my guidebook: the Villa Kerylos, a reconstruction of a typical homestead of the Greeks of antiquity, so it was claimed, and devised and inevitably financed by another eccentric Rothschild. It was less pretty than the Villa Ephrussi; on the other hand it was not the consequence of a temporary craze, for these Rothschilds had apparently lived in the house notwithstanding the primitive amenities and extreme discomfort. Was it mere coincidence that they were within easy reach of the five-star Hotel de Paris in Monte Carlo?

I turned left, walked for a quarter of an hour, passed the Villa Valerie behind its baobab tree and cloaked in shade and mist, and descended some steps to the bay of Villefranche. I was at the end of a cul-de-sac, for the pedestrian *Promenade des Marinières* alongside the road led only to a car park and a space where *boules* was played. The inlet of sea filled a loop gouged out of the lands of Cap Ferrat and Mont Boron. The railway line along which the trains whooshed – audibly from Gerbert's library – had kept the property developers at a discreet distance from the shoreline. The buildings opposite me, a few blocks of modern flats disproportionately tall, merged with the unspoilt *vieille ville* around the harbour, the shuttered houses painted turquoise and umber, the striped awnings of restaurants beyond the embankment, the bell-tower of the church in a dominant position, and the remains of a castle on a shoulder of the mountain.

I duly promenaded. Families were encamped on the sand just below me, and children and dogs frolicked and romped in the sparkling wavelets. Overlooking the little harbour there was a raised terrace, a square that was far from square, near a hotel called Welcome, and steps led uphill between the cafes with their chairs in the sun and their patrons imbibing elevenses. A street or alley at a higher level was shaded and cool, and the tantalising scent of baking wafted through it. I forced myself to buy only a street-map and climbed more steps to a part of the town like towns everywhere, replete with traffic and noise.

Chronologically it was now past midday, and I could yield without a guilty conscience to temptation. I returned to the alley, bought two hot crisp rolls in that bakery and in another shop salami and an orange, and repaired to a hilly rock garden and an empty seat and devoured my lunch.

The garden seemed to belong to the castle, which my map told me was known as *La Citadelle*. From it I looked down on the bustling waiters serving food and drinks in the square, and on the harbour, where a few rowing and fishing boats gently bobbed at anchor – the anchored yachts in the more open sea rocked in the swell. My map dignified the harbour with the name of port, *Port de la Santé* – but the French word means haven as well as port in the English sense. Could a full translation really be Haven of Health?

I had read that Nice and its environs had once been part of Italy, of Savoy to be precise. Nice itself had then been Nizza and Villefranche Villafranca; and it dawned on me that the name of the café where I telephoned Grace, *L'Elisir*, must derive from Donizetti's opera *L'Elisir d'Amore*. How peculiar, I reflected, munching my delectable repast of fresh bread and salami in the warm winter sunshine, that I had been drawn to places boasting respectively that they were an elixir and a healthy haven as soon as I could get away from the Villa Valerie!

I looked across the bay and thought I could see Gerbert's shady hideout under the evergreen trees. Its interior did not suffer only from the age of its occupant and owner, and the faint scent of sickness and decay. The atmosphere was uneasy, even stifling, and an extrasensory compass had possibly guided me to the sources of counteraction and replenishment.

Nonsense, I decided. Common sense reasserted itself. The Villa Valerie was not haunted – probably nowhere was, although I had a sneaking belief in the existence of ghosts. Gerbert was not an associate of the devil, he had been a hard-working self-made man, had stooped to conquer in the materialistic sense, as the newly rich have done ever since money was invented, and, with his more moral tales, was trying to set his record straight at half past eleven by the clock of fate.

Admittedly he had an inhuman air, but it must be attributable to anno domini, medicine and massage. I determined not to let superstition enter into our business dealings, nor to be overawed by his reputation and wealth, by the beauty of his home and the chilly remoteness of his personality.

But I could not help comparing his home with this venerable part of Villefranche, and with the human warmth stored down there by the lives of untold generations who had loved the place, now added to by the crowd in the so-called square, eating, drinking, laughing and basking in the sun.

In the library at six o'clock Gerbert said: 'In the beginning was the word, according to the Bible – a sentence most gratifying to scribes. But the words that govern civilised existence are euphemisms: justice, for instance, actually describes a compromise between truth and opinion, or democracy, another compromise by means of which we flatter and control the masses. Compromises are better than nothing – and what the relevant compromises are better than is nature ruthlessly red in tooth and claw.

'We have to defend ourselves against it. Civilisation is the veil we draw across the pain of life and death. We have to convince ourselves that we're superior to the brutality of the natural kingdom. But we step too far out of line at our peril. If with the aid of science we seize the initiative from nature, breaking its laws and evading its sanctions, for instance by aborting the next generation for the sake of sexual pleasure, we can expect none of the mercy or, to put it another way, of the feebleness of our human judiciary.

'Pestilence and drought are amongst nature's replies to our presumption. The dinosaurs got it in the neck for somehow offending the powers-that-be. Inconsistency may well be a punishable offence: science would save the lives of the ill and the old while it takes the lives of healthy unborn replacements. As for politics and politicians, they have signed the death warrants of innocent babies, yet keep the cruellest criminals in comfort and security for years and years at enormous cost to every law-abiding taxpayer in the land.

'Yesterday evening I talked about feminism, another breeding-ground of confusion. Women were not endowed with the physical fitness for motherhood in order that they should become pugilists and truck drivers. They are not the equals of men just as men are not their equals. They are very ignorant or very stupid to imagine that the opposite sex is not opposite in the sexual sense.

'But God knows, and history, physiology, the police, lawyers, hospitals and the divorce courts know that women need to be protected, and feminism, notwithstanding its counterproductive effects, does attempt to protect them and may to some extent succeed.

'My John and Felicity exemplified the mockery of nature that gets people into trouble. He was one of the fairly clever men who are twisted round the little fingers of half-witted women, and she paid the price of begetting a child by a travesty of the natural process. I did not finish their story – they were of no further interest. They were merely two more pieces of flotsam on the tide of folly and fashion, or another couple of volunteers for the great army of expendables by nature's criteria.

'Caroline was different. She lived and breathed and became my friend, although she too was a casualty of the precipitous road to love. She died young of cancer – she seemed younger than her fifty-odd years at the time of her death.

'The upshot of her experiences was her funeral in the English church in Nice some years ago, a sad occasion, a celebration of waste. Her husband Stas, short for Stanislaus, was present at the ceremony and behaved typically. He was Albanian or Bulgarian and, although no churchgoer, pointedly refused the offer of earth to throw into the grave and would not shake the hand of the vicar. He might have been drunk – he certainly was drunk at the wake in the house near Antibes where he had lived with Caroline.

'My last sight of her still vivid self was in a church, another church, oddly enough. We were attending the wedding of the daughter of mutual friends, more English refugees, and she was wearing a fortune on her back, as we used to say about well-dressed women. She loved clothes – perish the thought of females who don't! – and she ceased to economise on them in her last years. She was always small and neat, but illness had done her one favour by enabling her to climb into the garments designed for weedy models. She wore a perfect coat and skirt and a hat that fitted snugly over her blonde hair and the pretty shape of her head.

'She was made up to the eyes, literally. Mascara and the rest of it helped to disguise her pallor, and her character in fully developed form lent her an unusual beauty, although she was always sweet-looking. She held herself so well, straight-backed and light-footed as ever, and smiled on all and sundry with ethereal courage and gaiety.

'Posture is our best defence against the ageing process, and can be acquired; bones, alas, are hereditary and not for sale – no surgeon has yet been able to reproduce the real thing. Caroline was born an aristocrat and showed it by, for instance, the refinement of her skeletal structure, formed by centuries of selective breeding in the lap of luxury.

'I never would demean myself by reading Karl Marx, but I understand that he excludes the aristocracy from his socio-economic fantasies and aims his virulent rancour at the middle class. He thus betrays one of his many limitations – he was no doubt an inverted snob like the majority of scribblers, the academic type in particular. Was he so ignorant as not to have heard of the blood-lines of the breeding of animals which seeks to produce excellence and often succeeds? Was he so prejudiced and blinkered as to ignore the historical achievements of representatives of the upper class, and not to notice the genius for survival of certain aristocratic families and houses?

'Marx was the son of a lawyer, and lawyers are trained and paid to run with the hare and to hunt with the hounds. My mother was an exceptionally honest woman and my father a straightforward working man, and I'm grateful to have inherited a belief in the existence of truth, and an ability to recognise and tell it. A proper aristocrat may be a rarity but takes a lot of beating – much care, thought, expense and specially time goes into making one. Caroline who could scarcely spell her name and knew very little of anything disproves Marxism, which left her out of its rigid classifications; for she was above class, a person of value meriting conservation, not to be swept off the face of the earth by intellectual hooligans and mass-murderers.

'She should not have been at that wedding, considering how ill she was. Nor should I for that matter, but my wife was the godmother of the bride and had dragged me there. Caroline was a social butterfly, and derived nourishment by fluttering from guest to guest in noisy rooms awash with alcohol and choked by tobacco smoke. Perhaps it was her popularity that was nourishing. Granted, she spread herself thinly, but she had unfailing reserves of enthusiasm and undiscriminating sympathy, she never tired of laughter and drama, and had more friends than anybody – best friends to boot. She also had enough money, a comfortable home, two satisfactory children, a daughter and son who were grown up and had returned to England, and endless relations who were fond if far away.

'The fly in the ointment of this last stage of the life of Caroline was Stas, her second husband.

'Stas would have been absurd if he had not been villainous. He was the archetypal beachcomber, wastrel, gigolo, adventurer and petty crook, trawling for bounty in and out of the blue sea of the South of France. He put on weight as his wife lost it: which may speak volumes about his temperament. He was now a hulk with flat black hair like patent leather, oily and dyed, clipped black eyebrows and a black moustache, pig's eyes, a mean mouth and a round red face like a harvest moon. His conversation was loud, platitudinous, heavily accented, undiplomatic and uncharitable, but his rudeness was feared and he had an ugly temper. His walk, insofar as he did walk anywhere, was feline, the prowl of a hunting cat, and he conveyed the impression intentionally or unintentionally that he had irons in the fire of high finance and connections with the dubious characters who infest the Côte d'Azur.

'To say he was a fly is an inaccuracy. He was a black cloud that had positioned itself over Caroline's fair head. Once, thirty years before, he might have been slim and lithe, a sportsman, a seducer, *"toujours prêt"*, as they say in the hairdressers' salons. No longer – he was *"prêt"* for nothing these days, except soaking up alcohol – he was the luxury one would have thought she had had too much of, the financial burden, for he was always on or near the rocks, the social liability, the shadow she lived in and could not dodge.

'Their marriage was increasingly horrific throughout the course of her illness. I will not dwell on her fear of dying: I disapprove of the morbidity of the end of the twentieth century.

Even before she fell ill she was sick of him. He contradicted everything she said, and his booming accusations that she was a so-and-so ruined many social occasions. But cancer tightened all the screws: reinforced the undertow of regret for the mistakes she had made, imposed limits on her escapist interludes in society, threw the two of them more together.

'They asked people in to meals and drinks, but he was as unpopular as she was popular. Nobody wanted to sit next or talk to him, he would end by cursing Caroline in various languages. She had recourse to the telephone in the long evenings she was forced to spend in his company – he listened to her conversations and bawled interjections. He was without pity. While she cried on the shoulders of her friends because she had received more bad medical news, he discussed her investments in his deafening voice.

'Sometimes she fled to friends' homes. Yet sooner or later she reclaimed her own, her house, her husband, her wifely duties and the renewed aggravation. Everybody, and perhaps she herself, blamed Stas for her steady deterioration and possibly for her disease. The weaker she grew, the more violent he became, hurling furniture at her as well as reproaches and occasionally slapping her. On the other hand she acknowledged that she could be awkward, annoying, temperamental, hysterical. She was either forgiving or ready for another round of their fray, she anyway returned to the devil she knew, and once had loved, believe it or not, and had been determined to marry.

'At that time, in that incomprehensible period, while she courted him instead of vice versa, he was not much better than he became, only a little soberer, a little less gross, but already boorish and on the make. She loved him all the same; and in his caddish way he confided in somebody that she had threatened to kill herself unless he popped the question.

'When she was an attractive youngish woman, healthy, well-connected, with independent means, a general favourite, a darling full of fun, why did she want to marry the brute?'

*

Gerbert resumed after dinner: 'Caroline had been married before – Stas, needless to say, had had a string of wives. Caroline's first husband and the father of her children was an Oxford don fifteen years older than she was: on her wedding day she was twenty and he was thirty-five. Alfred was a different sort of disaster from Stas. He was a pale soft-haired blond, soft-handed, soft-spoken, a superior being who specialised in Eng. Lit. and was apt to stray into debutante dances. His fancy was to have romantic friendships with upper-class girls and blind them with the science of his erudition. Caroline could not believe it, and with reason. She knew she was a dunce, and Alfred refrained from correcting her idea that he was a genius. She lacked confidence, experience, knowledge of men and sex, of the way of the world and the snares along it. She was a late developer, an elf, a sprite with social advantages, and as such, as she at any rate appeared to be, she suited Alfred. He proposed and she accepted him almost before he had finished speaking.

'Her family began by objecting to her choice or his, the age difference, the absence of interests in common. But just at the end of the prolonged engagement, when Caroline told members of her family that she could not go through with her wedding, they compounded their error with interest by telling her she could not possibly back out.

'She had changed her mind in bed with Alfred. She had surrendered her virginity reluctantly, or, rather, he had eventually and without much conviction claimed it. She might be stupid, but was not persuaded that passion was so lukewarm and limp. She recoiled from the prospect of innumerable nights fraught with embarrassment and frustration. Eng. Lit. was less important than she had thought it was, and she realised that for Alfred's sake she was about to reject a cornucopia of opportunities.

'However, good manners took precedence over good sense, noblesse obliged, she yielded to family pressure and bowed to convention, and lived more or less unhappily not exactly ever after but in North Oxford.

'She made the best of a bad job in and out of bed, and was

busy with her children. She was dutiful, and he did quite well at his work and kept a roof over their heads. They had their circle of acquaintance, dingy as it was, they attended functions, they spent his annual holiday at seaside resorts on the east coast, and rubbed along for a decade and a half. Sometimes his mildness infuriated her, sometimes she felt she was being ground into the dust by the terrible strength of the weak, and by his hypocritical egoism. Then she would have to apologise for her desperate outbursts. She grew ever more aware of a wider world than hers, where her social equals revelled in gracious circumstances, and fine specimens of manhood romped with forward girls.

'She reached the age of thirty-five without acceding to the propositions of Lotharios in mortarboard and gown. She was introduced to James by her sister at a polo match at Cirencester. He had been playing polo, he was apparently a rich man, and he now looked hot and handsome. And he was also taller and stronger than Alfred, and had bluer eyes, whiter teeth and a more commanding presence. He made her feel wistful; but he too was married.

'A few days later he rang her up – luckily Alfred was out of the house. James was going to be in Oxford and wanted her to lunch with him. It was like an order, and in her astonishment the idea of disobeying it did not cross her mind. She omitted to inform Alfred of the plan. Despite her unwonted excitement, she half-wished James had not tracked her down.

'They met in a swish hotel in the country, and were the only customers in its restaurant. Over the first course he said he had fallen in love with her at first sight, and over the pudding that he had booked a room in the hotel where they could be alone. She could not protest, she had eaten nothing, she seemed to be paralysed although she was able to follow him upstairs, and her heart beat frantically.

'The experience was in all respects new to her. The wonder of it, and her wide-eyed gratitude, stimulated both of them. The vows they exchanged were as abandoned as their physical communion. They parted late in the day, and were too bemused to fix another meeting.

'Her dream of love became nightmarish when she contemplated in relative tranquillity the professional expertise of her seduction. He knew the ropes all too well, and who else was he lassoing with his dashing looks and uninhibited declarations? But James rang again and dispelled her suspicions and fears. He wished to know when they could safely talk on the telephone, and persuaded her to meet him in London.

'Adultery put forth its buds and blossom. He was a landowner and gentleman about town, and not happy with his wife, who was bossy and bad-tempered. Caroline admitted she was bored to tears by Alfred, and had realised that his braininess meant nothing to her and his middle-class code of conduct grated. But James added that his spouse was not a bad person or a bad mother of their children, and Caroline that hers might have been worse.

'The sharp thorns that grew alongside the flowers of extramarital love began to draw blood. Caroline missed the embraces of James. Although he rang her constantly, she missed the sound of his voice on the telephone. Her boredom with Alfred, who stood between her and the object of her desire, turned into hostility. Why, Alfred asked her, and then, what was going on? Having to lie to him did not make her love him any better. He refused to accept her excuses for sleeping in their spare room, and claimed his rights against her will and almost sacrilegiously in her view. One day he came home unexpectedly and heard her talking to James.

'A dreadful row ensued. Alfred was beside himself – she had not known he could be so angry. When she owned up and defied him, he thumped her on the chest and the pain reduced her to tears that were rebellious. She seized her first opportunity to tell James, who issued threats to maim or kill Alfred. Oh no, she said – she was sorry to have worried him – she would work things out for the sake of her children – and the same applied in his marriage.

'But Alfred was vain and cowardly. He was offended that Caroline preferred another man, and he hit and hurt and bruised her where it did not show instead of confronting James. He spurned olive branches and made out she was mad. Sometimes he begged her in unbecoming terms to see sense, and when she was slow to answer, before she had had time to disguise her revulsion and to think of a diplomatic response, he would rant and rage and reduce her to tears. She was not equipped to cope with the maelstrom of her own emotions and the conflicting passions of two men. She could not stop crying in conversations with her lover and in his company. In desperation or exasperation he said they would have to seek divorces and marry each other.

'It was the only thing to do, he said in his impetuous way. He boiled his arguments down to bare essentials. He could not let her be murdered by her husband, and he wanted to spend the rest of his life with her. Therefore she must get rid of Alfred while he extricated himself from his marriage. The consequences would be her safety and his happiness: she would be granted custody of her children because of Alfred's violence; the abandoned ones would be much better off without spouses who hated them; and all would be well.

'She trusted him – he was so authoritative and attractive. She had no one else to be guided by. She wrote a letter to Alfred, decamped into a rented flat in London with her children, engaged the sympathy of her family by saying she was a refugee from assault and battery, and instructed a solicitor.

'She found herself entangled in the law. Apparently, because she had vacated the marital home of her own volition, she was in danger of being divorced for desertion and losing her children and her home, unless she brought a case of cruelty against her husband and won it. She could not follow the legal jargon, and she did not see enough of James. She suffered from dread, loneliness, guilt because of her unsettled children, and pangs of compassion for Alfred and his opposite number. She was contrarily relieved to hear that James had not yet broken the news to his wife that he was leaving her.

'Her solicitor probed into her intimate marital relations, and extracted answers from her that were incriminating and half the truth. She began to receive terrible letters and telephone calls from Alfred, who was deeply affronted by her solicitor's communications. She lied to her family about her marriage and put the blame on Alfred so that James would not be blamed. She felt that events were no longer controllable – her life was out of control.

'And she clung to James. Even she knew she should not cling, but she did. Unfortunately, he explained, he had to keep a long-standing engagement to play polo in Argentina. He posted his note at the airport to say he could not and would not divorce his wife.

'Caroline was shattered utterly. She dropped all legal proceedings, and was duly divorced for desertion. Alfred was unforgiving and restricted her access to her children, of whom he had been awarded custody. She wanted to hide from her family and friends, and hoped that her children would love her better if she could provide holiday fun for them in the South of France. She emigrated and she married Stas.'

'You can't legislate for fools, any more than you can legislate against poverty,' Gerbert decreed sternly. 'But Caroline, although she was not good at her books and had no intellectual interests or general knowledge, confined most of her foolishness within the parameters of her dealings with men: she picked badly and was picked on. Otherwise she was a competent quick-witted person.

'To delve deeper than Stas, James and Alfred into her biography is to encounter her father, her aristocratic sire, a distinguished man by all accounts, charming when he was sober, irate and unkind to her at other times.

'Uncertainty is cruel to children. They need to know where they stand. Felicity who thought a turkey-baster was as good as a father was wrong: children need to know their daddy and especially to know that they have one. And in the case of girls, with any luck daddy will win their love and retain it, and set an example of benign masculinity to guide them through the marriage market. A tipsy father has the opposite effect, for he is nice and nasty for no known reason, confuses and can frighten his daughters, and provides misleading evidence by which they will judge their suitors.

'Caroline's father again did wrong in her young eyes by dying young and seeming to leave her in the lurch. Her upbringing thereafter lacked any intimate masculine influence, for she had no brother – two sisters but no brother to accustom her to the male physique and mentality, and to instruct in the management of the same.

'Moreover she was sent to a school run on avant-garde lines. Although she never told me so, I suspect she was an early victim of the craze that goes by the name of sex education. Modernists have persuaded themselves that, by teaching children how to copulate, the children will refrain from copulating. But childish psychology often does what it's told not to do: everybody knows it, except the intelligentsia. The result is that schoolgirls nowadays are either terrified of the sexual realities or get pregnant.

'Teaching is an art, and good teachers are as rare as good writers. Imagine public lessons in sex by the bad teachers we can all remember! They must have wrecked the sex lives of numberless sensitive souls. And talk of putting the cart before the horse! Children should be informed in school of the beautiful ideal of love, enshrined in religion, and expressing itself in the complete union of a man and woman that leads by way of their physical exchange to the gift of life to offspring. To aim less high, tuition should at least describe the dangers – for a girl – of falling for a man much older than she is, or already married, or of a different race or class, or with a bad temper, and for a boy of running the applicable obvious risks.

'I digress, forgive me!

'Caroline's luck was patchy. She was well-bred, good-natured, attractive, and not poor; yet in the context of love and marriage she did not have much fun, and she succumbed to cancer in her fifties. I was sorry for her, everyone was, and we mourned and missed her.

'But luck is usually an alloy of good and bad. And nature is not so sentimental as we are. Although our Maker is said to imbue us with the faculty and the freedom to err, the same arbiter of our existence has no pity upon us for erring. Perhaps Caroline was overburdened by the sins of her father. Nevertheless the rest of her life, her healthy life, was like Felicity's in that it was her own fault. She was infinitely superior to Felicity, but how could she have entrusted herself to those appalling men? If discrimination is one of the tests set by nature, she could not very well have been selected to survive. And she fell foul of the implacable law laid down by Jesus in the parable of the talents: "from him that hath not shall be taken away even that which he hath".

'I am not heartless. I would rather say to the next generation "Beware!" than "I told you so!" '

Matrimonial

I left the Villa Valerie early the next day. I was not going home, but could not wait to get out of the house. I walked to Villefranche and caught the minibus at the Haven of Health for Nice.

The sunshine was restorative. It was like that power of good which chases away the hobgoblins and demons of the night in myth and legend. The bus climbed uphill and round the side of Mont Boron and after three or four miles provided a bird's-eye view of the city reaching round and back from its angelic bay; and the angels that surely designed it seemed to flutter their wings and free me from Gerbert's spell.

At Nice, modernisers have for once failed to deface a fine landscape. The curve of the bay is intact, not ruined by the spit of land reclaimed from the sea for airport runways at one end, nor noticeably affected by the old harbour and new marina at the other. Can the Bay of Naples be better? Here cars speed to and fro on a six-lane motorway between the *Promenade des Anglais* and the grand hotels, but at least they do not stray on to the beach, and roadside palm trees and flowers soften their visual impact.

Our driver, having swung his bus round hairpin bends above precipices, now had a go at the traffic jams. He was brave or foolhardy, but cheerful enough to make me hope he was a descendant of the first best chauffeurs who were always French. He drew up in a bus station where the diesel fumes posed another danger. I emerged and crossed the road and survived to find myself in a market selling fish and food, where a signpost directed me to the flower market nearer the sea.

I walked through the alleys and canyons of this *vieille ville*. The sun could not squeeze between the tall black buildings seeming almost to touch at the top. The air that would have been cool in the shade in summer was now decidedly wintry. Cavernous doorways, humble shops lit by bare bulbs, hobbling pensioners in bedroom slippers, boys on bicycles skidding between the pedestrians – the scene was Dickensian with a foreign flavour. A smell of cooking emanated from a typical thieves' kitchen with a dusty black curtain looped across its cracked windowpanes.

I grew apprehensive. Momentarily I associated present darkness with that in which Gerbert spun his yarns and his webs. I wondered whether I was about to be mugged – the sinister side of things was uppermost in my mind. But the last alley ushered me into open space and blue sky with the sun steadfast in heaven, and stalls of flowers under awnings in lines, flowers in pots on the ground, flowers being sold, bought and carried home, and the scent of flowers mixing with the ozone.

I was in a marketplace where vegetables were also for sale, and the chairs and tables outside the countless restaurants were occupied by some of the crowd of shoppers, consuming the elevenses favoured by the French, knock-out coffee laced with cognac, for example. Everybody appeared to be composed and content: my impression that the natives were jollier, or at any rate took their pleasure less sadly and grimly, than their Nordic counterparts was confirmed. I mingled and edged through on the lookout for a telephone box where I might be able to speak to Grace.

It was no use. In the phone box I began by failing to follow the instructions and finished by not getting an answer to my call, and then ran out of the correct money. The difficulties did not matter much: Grace had told me she was meaning to drive Oliver to visit distant friends, and I had told her I might ring too late to catch her – we had agreed not to worry if we were unable to speak during the day. Although I did worry, naturally, I wanted time on neutral ground in which to cogitate.

There had been trouble in the night. My bedroom at the Villa Valerie looked east, away from the sea and towards the baobab tree. It was large and luxurious, filled with highly polished old furniture and heavily curtained, and had an adjoining bathroom virtually made of marble. The curtains on the two windows were light-proof and air-proof, and, since Grace and I opt for maximum exposure to the elements, I never drew them. I was consequently woken at two o'clock in the morning by an unprecedented blinding brightness.

I stumbled across to a window. Powerful security lights blazed away at the entrance gates and everywhere else so far as I could see, all along the perimeter wall and on the roof of the house. A car was coming up the drive at speed with its headlights also dazzling me as it turned corners. It stopped by the front door, and two men stepped out, Lee who must have hitched a ride from the lodge and a grey-haired man carrying an unmistakable rectangular black doctor's bag.

Gerbert was ill surely. I doubted that a doctor would have been summoned in the depths of the night, or would have responded to such a summons, to attend any alien who was not an international notability. Gerbert was dying – again, patients in their eighties who succeed in calling out medical assistance in the smaller hours are unlikely to survive.

The house was as quiet as the grave. My first thoughts were not materialistic. I expected lightning and thunder to mark his passing and did not count the cost to me personally. Would the devil let him go, I wondered, and would the jaws of hell open to receive him and, incidentally, myself? Then I got a grip of reality and recognised my surprising sensations of regret.

I regretted the likely fact that our last combined literary effort would come to nought. I was disappointed that I would probably never hear another extraordinary soliloquy, story, chapter or discourse delivered in that harmonious voice. I was sorry not to have solved the riddle of Gerbert, and, to put it more simply, I wanted him not to die just yet. Not that I liked him much, not that I was altogether convinced by the pornographer turned preacher, not that I could summon up many good words for him by conventional standards; but he was more of an artist than I had expected, and he had seemed to me to have a touch of immortality.

At any rate I realised that I owed him something as well as being owed: although I was not clear as to the form of the book he wished me to write, and uncertain that I was equal to the task of putting his idea of the ascending levels of love into publishable words, he had reintroduced me to the creative shivers down my scribbler's backbone which I had imagined and been afraid I would never know again.

I went back to bed and lay awake, listening. The lights of another car shone on my bedroom ceiling. I returned to the window and saw and heard a police car crunching across the gravel sweep. A uniformed officer emerged from the car and at the same time a female figure in white bustled out of the front door below me – not Marie – Marie's mother, who was stouter. Had Gerbert been murdered? Had burglars broken in? Voices were raised, a Frenchman's and an Indonesian woman's, and the two people on the doorstep were gesticulating and trying to make themselves understood. Now Mrs Lee was waving the policeman away, and he re-entered the car, which coasted down the drive and off the premises – the gates were workable from the Villa and from its lodge, where Lee's gardening brother might be playing a part in the proceedings.

I waited by the window. Suddenly all the lights went out. My immediate startled superstitious deduction was that Gerbert had died – I fancied the electricity company had been prevailed upon by hook or crook to mark his passing. But common sense reasserted itself and reminded me that security lights were controlled by timing devices. The night seemed darker than dark, and I could hear nothing inside or outside the house.

Then the front door opened, a shaft of yellow light cut through the blackness, the doctor appeared with Mrs Lee in tow, spoke to her for a moment and shook his head – because Gerbert was past praying for, or because they could not communicate? – and hurried to his car. The security lights did not come on again – somewhere there must have been an overriding switch. The red rearlights of the doctor's car vanished behind the baobab, and the not very ghostly white shape of Mrs Lee waddled indoors and shut the front door.

Another unanswered question kept me awake. What had Lee been doing at the far end of the garden in the middle of the night – where exactly did the Lees sleep?

At six o'clock I had a bath and decided to see Nice before flying home. I was assuming that Gerbert was either deceased or too ill to talk to me. Thoughts of the ten thousand pounds I was unlikely to be paid crossed my mind – and, reflecting Gerbert's moralistic influence, I remembered that when writers agree to write for money not strictly needed they offend their muse, who is unforgiving.

But downstairs at seven-thirty or eight both Lees, Mr and Mrs, greeted me with their customary smiles and ushered me into the dining-room for breakfast. They would not answer, they refused to understand, my questions. Sir Gerbert? They nodded affirmatively. He was okay? They laughed at my suggestion that he was not. *Le patron*? More nods. *Est-il bien*? More laughter. Then Mrs Lee smote her forehead with her hand, retired to the kitchen and returned with a piece of flapping paper similar to the one Marie had presented on the day of my arrival. She gave it to me and I read in Gerbert's spidery writing: *'A l'heure sacrée du cocktail!'*

I was relieved or irritated, I scarcely knew which. To cut the story short, I walked out of the house and, in a matter of an hour or so, into a better and certainly more straightforward world of flowers.

In Nice, after wandering through the flower market, I crossed the dual carriageway along which Lee had driven me from the airport, and began to walk along the several miles of the *Promenade des Anglais*. The Mediterranean sea scintillated and stroked the shore on my left hand side, and on my right were the grandiose opera house gardens, a casino, hotels of all ages, apartment blocks and the famous Negresco Hotel with its turquoise dome and costumed commissionaires. The people of Nice were taking the air on the strip of tarmac some twenty yards wide. They pushed aged relations in wheelchairs and babies in prams. They strapped babies to their chests, and guided toddlers in harness. They had arms round shoulders and waists, were arm-in-arm, held hands, and had their hands in one another's back pockets. They wore fur coats or T-shirts. They led dogs, *le fox*, poodles, and the shepherding breeds of Northern Europe commonly and incorrectly called Alsatians.

The latter made me feel the more homesick. I yearned for Crystal as well as Grace. Dogs like Crystal were good, but bad human beings have introduced faults into the breed either deliberately or moronically, hopeless hindquarters which are all the rage, madness due to inbreeding, neuroses and painful physical defects that ruin tempers. There are many more nasty owners of every sort of dog than nasty dogs which have been treated nicely. The canine population of the Côte d'Azur seemed to be lucky. The eyes of dogs are their autobiographies: those with which I exchanged glances reminded me of Crystal's.

I suppose I should not write in praise of dogs in general and my own in particular: dog-haters exist, and I have been friendly with some of them. Yet I cannot help recording my nostalgia for the mild wise gaze of Crystal's brown eyes fixed upon mine, the affection in them and the sympathy; and, as I promenaded, that memory reminded me with an even sharper pang of Grace's incomparable regard.

On the subject of eyes, a reflection that was disturbing in a different way struck me. I wished Gerbert would remove his dark spectacles, so that I could perhaps understand him.

He was already in the library at six o'clock, and Marie sat as usual by the two bottles of wine. He again wore his dark glasses, and he bade me good evening in what seemed to be a repressive tone. Marie smiled without looking at me when I addressed her.

The lamp on the desk cast its circle of radiance, but did not reveal any special signs of frailty in Gerbert's countenance.

'You received my message?' he asked, and, when I said yes,

he vouchsafed a pleasantry on the cocktail theme. 'Will you make do with wine?'

Marie came and offered me my glass on her knees. Her shy modesty, the lissom movements of her youth, were extremely appealing.

I ventured to express the hope that all was well.

'As well as can be expected,' he replied. 'Why do you ask?'

I hesitated. He was a tough customer and no mistake. He seemed to want to make me say that I had been afraid he was at death's door. But I was not going to pay him the compliment of confessing that I cared, nor would I let him think I had been worried about my fee.

'Cars were rolling up the drive in the small hours,' I half-explained.

'I apologise for the disturbance,' he commented blandly. Then it was as if he dropped his guard. 'I wrote you a note in case you jumped to the conclusion that I'd be underground by now. One foot is already there, but no more of me than that. Your sleep was sacrificed on the altar of my sawbones. The act of creation is apt to be exciting, and the excitement of yesterday, of literary composition, strained my physical resources. My attendants summoned Docteur Palin, and I understand the police noticed the lights for burglars to see by and barged in. I'm sorry.'

'And I'm glad you're better.'

'I wasn't really worse. It was the faintest swish of the scythe of the grisly reaper that was heard. Authors can't afford to be unwell in the middle of their most important books – and I consider that I'm talking a book, whether or not you agree.'

I volunteered a pacific reply.

'With respect,' he began ominously, 'and your good self excepted, authors and artists are the curse of humanity. They were my heroes, they were my saints, but I have come round to believing that the ones who make the deepest impressions are the deadliest. Wait, please – I'll elaborate in a moment! To continue to generalise, we artists, we authors, have one virtue: we work hard, we work for low pay or no pay, we are dogged by demons if we don't, illness and old age do not excuse us, resignation and retirement are out of bounds, and death itself has to wait for the last of our full stops.'

I laughed at this spirited rigmarole.

'But,' he as it were recalled me to the serious side of things, 'that virtue is also our vice. We write too much. We write for effect, and discretion and restraint, obligations, consequences, count for nothing. I speak from experience and with feelings of guilt, although I am a minnow in a pool of sharks. The downside of the Bible has been two thousand years of conflict. The author of *Das Kapital* has so far drowned one century in blood. And Sigmund Freud was the worst of the lot. Freud assured us scientifically that we were not to blame for anything – war, genocide, the holocaust, the gulags, crime and abortion – the villain of the piece is our unconscious motivation, which is not controllable.'

He broke off to cough. He did seem weaker than he had been, he had difficulty in clearing his throat. But when Marie rose to attend to him he signalled that she was only to replenish our glasses.

He resumed: 'The archetypal author was the serpent in the Garden of Eden, which told Eve more than was good for her to know. Ever since, to a greater or lesser degree, authors have hissed out destructive information. Christian teaching sanctioned conversion by force. Rousseau's drivel set the tumbrils rolling toward the Napoleonic wars. Marx's Manifesto turned man against man. Meanwhile novelists were secularising, popularising, sensationalising and, I would say, dissecting love until there was damn-all left of it.

'I exaggerate. Haste and conviction combine together to overegg my arguments. Love, like the novel, exists after all. Life on earth equals nature, and nature equals love in reproductive mode. Youth is still ardent even if the end of the world is nigh. But authorship has changed its mind; literary snobbery has inverted; today's hero is the working man, working in principle if not in practice; and the fashionable etiquette reduces love to its lowest common denominator. Refined feelings, the search for the reciprocation of affection, cautious commitment and unswerving fidelity are out, are considered off-puttingly posh and as old hat as good manners. The replacement, what is in, is love in the form that media people tell us that the workers make it, sexually, promiscuously, carelessly, brutally.

'Therefore marriage is discouraged because it restrains and disciplines. I understand that in England today even the establishment puts obstacles in the matrimonial path: the taxes are higher for couples who elect not to live in sin, as we used to say, and the divorce laws are the new Eldorado for gold-diggers.

'You might think I have no right to discuss the merits of marriage. I would plead that I have more experience of the married state than the average, and that poachers make the best gamekeepers. And I object to the unconventional conventions in force just as I objected to the stuffy and straitlaced punctilio of yesteryear.

'Although love may not cast out fear, it should at least overcome the fearful anticipation of marital failure. Ideally no intersexual relationship should be entered into on the basis that the partners cannot trust each other; and everyone would be well advised to give the widest berth to men and women who do not trust themselves. At the same time mutual love that is true is not blind: it sees that a framework of support is needed to preserve the essential confidence of both parties and the safety and wellbeing of their issue. To reject the assistance of tradition and the law must mean either that you don't care or that you're foolhardy. Love that disbelieves in the torments of jealousy, that disregards the powers of temptation, that sits back complacently and does not expect passion to transmute or time to pass, is in for rude shocks. Successful, reciprocal, lasting love is wary and alive to danger, and would bind the beloved to itself by vows, prayers, ceremonies, social pressure, financial tie-ups and legal implications.

'Liberals who have faith in free love would say I was cynical, as I would say that the hopes of liberals are always unrealistic. It can't be cynical for lovers to reject the philosophy of impermanence, to wish to make the most serious of all commitments, to ask for their exchange of vows to be witnessed and reinforced by religion, and in short to embrace for themselves the method recommended by civilisations of creating the maximum happiness for the greatest number of people.'

After supper Gerbert resumed: 'More murders are committed in marital homes than anywhere else, the newspapers tell us with relish. I too could give you a hundred good reasons never to tie the knot, and I'm sure you could do the same. What is wrong, what can go wrong, with marriage is obvious and indisputable. But we can leave it to the journalists to accentuate the negative. The last and the hardest of the struggles of life is not to lose hold of optimism.

'However, contrarily, with autobiographical contrariness, I would speak of friends of mine who created a little hell of their own on earth. It was near here, at Roquebrune; and to be equally precise she was my friend, he was not. They were intelligent sophisticated people and lived graciously; they broke no written laws and were convicted of no crimes. They were called Yves and Martine, a gilded couple, popular, well-to-do, with houses in Paris and in the Swiss mountains. They had an only child, a daughter, Léonie by name, who was about six years old when I got to know the family.

'Martine was nearly half a century younger than I was at the time of our meeting. She was a type of woman that exists only in France, a national treasure, a typical individualist in paradoxical terms. In her thirties she was elegant, spirited, cultivated, seductive – *avec du chien,* as her compatriots say, meaning with the instinctive spontaneity and appetites of a dog. She had perfect taste and had read everything, yet was not a bluestocking in the daunting dowdy English tradition, nor, for that matter, a *précieuse ridicule* in the French. She was at once refined and reserved and warm-hearted and jolly, and appealed to everybody, both sexes, all classes, most children, animals.

'But Yves was, or considered himself, or was considered by some, the beauty. He had an aquiline profile, thick silver hair, a slim figure and a permanent suntan. He was also well-informed and shrewd and apparently successful in his work at an international bank. Needless to say he was spoilt to death by women. He was too French for me, too much of a peacock, and his conduct was unbecoming and its effects thoroughly disagreeable. The house at Roquebrune was inherited – his money was old as well as new. It was luxurious and, perched on top of the hill, had tremendous views. He seemed to have lots of time to spend there, sunning himself.

'I was never Martine's lover in the technical sense, but our friendship had its passionate moments. If I'd been younger the story would have been different – we both knew that, it spiced our relations, and the fact that each of us was at ease with the opposite sex cut corners. At first our link was literature. She'd read my books. She wrote to me in English – she was fluent in English – to wonder if I would do her the honour of coming to lunch. I went, saw and was conquered. I was the more drawn to her because she behaved as well as Yves behaved badly.

'It was a South of France party – I speak pejoratively. On arrival, I was ushered through the house by a white-jacketed butler and out and down garden steps to a terrace with a swimming pool. My heart sank: I smelt ladies' perfume and tobacco smoke instead of flowers, and heard brazen voices and laughter and the dread sound of bathers shrieking and splashing. They were swimming and drinking and lying round the pool in varying states of undress in the blinding sunlight, a dozen or so, while the child Léonie sat on her father's lap.

'Martine wore a flimsy flowing garment, tantalising yet discreet – her appearance was more appealing than the oily female flesh on display. She shook hands in the right way, just as later she kissed platonically with meaning and without haste or shyness. It was friendship at first sight. She said to me, "My husband has asked some neighbours to join us" – an exemplary instance of tact, since she was confiding in me and implying that she had hoped to have me more to herself, and at the same time being neither inhospitable nor disloyal. Yves did not rise to his feet when she introduced us, a breach of the code of good manners in France, not to mention the respect owed to seniority. He pretended he was pinned down by his daughter and extended a languid hand – incidentally he was bilingual. When he instructed Léonie to greet me and she pouted and averted her head and pushed her face against his naked chest, instead of checking her he laughed – they both sniggered conspiratorially.

'He ordered Martine to introduce me to the others, fix me a drink, replenish everyone's glasses, fetch dry towels for the swimmers, see if lunch was ready. He lounged and laughed at her with Léonie, then called her his *pauvre petite* and accused himself of being a martinet and a cruel taskmaster. The other ladies of a certain age, bulging out of their bikinis, thought he was funny. Martine did as she was told, her patience was admirable; but after I had grilled in the sun for ten minutes she brought me a spare sun-hat and looked at me with an expression that subtly combined apology and exasperation.

'We had lunch at last under a pergola in the blessed shade. The female guests had covered their nakedness, and the men wore shirts over their bathing trunks. Amongst the oddities of Yves was that he had the head of an aesthete and the stout legs of a banker who would relish the task of telling his customers they were overdrawn. But the oddity did not stop there.

'He seemed to be intent on, and to derive amusement from, teasing his wife. Although the food was exquisite, his interrogative whining carried the length of the table to where Martine sat at the other end. For my benefit, that is to embarrass her in front of me, he inquired in his English with its Gallic tang: "What are we meant to be eating? . . . How are we meant to eat it? . . . This meat is tough – it is more for the soles of shoes than for a famous writer . . . Why won't you take more interest in the kitchen? You have your head in the clouds, *ma pauvre petite*!"

'His flirting with the ladies on his right and left was impossible to ignore. When he was feeding one of them with a forkful from his own plate he called out: "Observe, Martine, what a nice time I'm having!" Giggling was interspersed with squeaks and squawks as they played games with hands and feet under the table. He turned Léonie into an instrument of torture. The child had been seated with her nurse at a separate small table, where she created more difficulties by mimicking her father's plaintiveness. Yves undermined Martine's attempts to exert parental discipline by summoning Léonie and consoling her with titbits of grown-up food and swigs of wine. Then he nagged the butler to such an extent that the flustered man laid down his dishes and fled in the middle of serving the pudding course – Martine had to do the job herself.

'Yves was not a boor. My description may create an impression of boorishness, but he was more feline. And he was able to present his inclination to torment his wife as humour, as the incorrigible characteristic of a superannuated naughty scamp of a boy. He was clearly considered a card by his guests: perhaps that was why he had invited them, as it were to defend him against Martine's – myself – who was more likely to be on her side. Towards the end of lunch he swapped chairs with a neighbour of mine and talked to me briefly. He said he was afraid he was not literary, nor as clever as his wife. He ruined the effect of this disarming statement by adding that he could not make head or tail of my books. I remember another gambit of his that cut both ways: he declared that he could never wait to get out of his office and into the sun of the south, and that he pitied me for living in such a gloomy pile.

'A sort of armistice was celebrated with the circulation of liqueurs and cigars. Martine instigated a move away from the table to easier chairs also in the shade, and she and I, sitting together, conversed more consecutively. She lost her taut wary look, she had no immediate reason to bite back wrathful retorts, she conveyed to me without interruptions the things that authors love to hear, and her enthusiasm for literature was fresh and touching.

'Yves soon objected. He asked her to read her poetry to the assembled company. He was thus invading the privacy she guarded closely, as I was later to learn, and making it as difficult as possible for her to repulse him. When she demurred, he drew attention to my qualifications to judge, criticise, amend and improve her poems, and suggested that her refusal to submit them to my arbitration amounted to a vote of no confidence in her pet author. He said her poetry would benefit from some severe editing, and led a chorus of requests for her to relent and provide postprandial entertainment.

'She was evidently mortified. She reminded me of a fine animal cornered by a predator – Yves' teasing seemed to have deteriorated into blood lust. He exchanged one term of ostensible endearment – *pauvre petite* – which was patronising and bad enough, for another – *pauvre poète* or *pauvre poétesse* – which was worse. He approached Martine as if to raise her from her chair by force, he had a nasty spiteful look in his eye although he was showing his teeth in a lupine smile. And he called her "Pipi" – he laughed and called her by the first letters of those pairs of words by which he liked to address her, the combination meaning in his native tongue "urine".

'She stood up of her own accord, took hold of my hand, said to me: "I'm sorry you have to leave us," and led me into the house. Her hot hand shook with emotion. Yves followed us, now wailing more than whining: wailing in French and English that it was merely a play on words, a joke, and what had he done wrong this time, and why was she so hard on him?

'At last she spoke her mind. Curtly, cuttingly, with the rapid delivery of a reproof I did not catch and probably would not have understood anyway, she punctured his balloon. Her temper was unexpectedly fierce, and his collapse likewise; but the least expected of his reactions was the pleasure he obviously derived from acting the part of a whipped cur. He squirmed and whimpered. He almost boasted to me that his wife was *méchante*. My impression was that he had got not only what he deserved but what he wanted.

'On one or two other occasions I returned to the house at Roquebrune when he was absent. We met elsewhere, Yves and I, and were polite to each other; but Martine had the tact to spare me the distress of witnessing his marital manners. She also chose days to invite me on which Léonie, who loved her father and treated her mother as he did, would not be making mischief. Those rooms with enviable views, that pretty space under the pergola, were still not conducive to relaxed conversation. The whole place had a bad atmosphere, and I was always relieved to depart, having obtained her acceptance of my invitations to visit me here.

'We would sit together on the long chairs under the pine trees, looking out at the sails of holiday boats on the open sea, and she began to confide in me – or should I say confess? She was more intelligent than Yves if not cleverer, and a talented individual even if her talent was not exactly poetic, but she retained the quality of girlish innocence which is an essential element of lovable womanhood – female know-alls are not much loved by men, and are hated by their own sex. It was innocent of her to think that because I had written about romance and the seamier side of it I could throw helpful light on her murky marriage. She turned to me as others turn to psychiatrists and used to turn to priests. She wanted to believe in fairy tales, she yearned for a miracle, and was hopeful that I would tell her how to live happily ever after.

'She understood so much, yet was at a loss. Her husband had muddled her, to put it mildly. She said almost in the same sentence that he was a sadist and kind and charitable. She could have killed him on the day I came to lunch, yet was sorry she had ended by speaking to him harshly and hurting his feelings. He was extraordinarily sensitive where he himself was concerned, she revealed, and he stepped on everybody else's toes without fail. He was treacherous, he lulled people into thinking he meant no harm, then snapped at them and drew blood; at the same time he was sweet to strangers, he could be protective, and she depended on him in many ways. He played cat to Léonie's mouse, too, indulging her at one moment and ignoring her the next, confusing her and wrecking her nervous system; and as in every other situation and circumstance he pulled against rather than with Martine, he conspired and worked against her and their family interests.

'He was a man who was bad for women. He looked good, made a beeline for the attractive ones, flirted to the limit and worked them up, then disappointed them and hid behind the skirts of his wife. His amorous technique was bravado, he was an unsatisfactory lover, he lashed out at the women he had deceived before he was lashed out at, his bullying was really cowardice. He had no fundamental confidence – was that his basic problem? I had seen him at his worst, she said, because he was jealous of more normal men, also jealous of success, especially of the successful writers and artists who were her friends, and felt at a disadvantage and punished her as a result, wishing to prove in public that he had the upper hand. But she was wrong to have crushed him – she was afraid that one day she would forget to remember how strong she was and destroy him or cause him to be self-destructive.

'Why had she married him? At too early an age she was orphaned and thrown into a world of predators, into a den of male lions, and she had no money and made mistakes in order to save her skin. When she met Yves she was at the end of her tether, and he liked that, he liked the idea that he could rescue her, and he was unattached, well-to-do, decent, pressing and impatient.

'I am not ungrateful, she said – he not only seemed to be my knight in shining armour, he was, he has been, he still is from objective points of view; he has given me his name, a child, a position in society, some security and some freedom to follow my star of poetry and art, although he puts every obstacle he can think of in the way of my literary interests and then scolds and mocks me for not working harder at my writing.

'She repeated my question – why? – and puzzled over an answer to it. She had married him not for her own gain – honestly! – but, when all was said, because she was afraid of what would happen to him if he lost her. Strange as it might sound, she said, she pitied him, and considered herself his guardian as in a sense he was hers, and that she must not disregard her responsibilities or abandon him to a fate that could be much crueller than the pinpricks she had to suffer matrimonially.

'My verdict, my response, was short if not sweet, and definitely not miraculous: I see, I commented, knowing better than to step voluntarily on the quicksands of somebody else's marriage.

'But Martine would not let me get away with it. She begged me to tell her the truth, what I really thought, what she should do, how she was to live and not to die of her predicament. She cajoled me, she wheedled. She showed her strength, the strength of her charm and determination, by eliciting opinions that might have been better kept to myself. Eventually I explained that she had stumbled into the trap set for superior people, who are apt to suffer from an excess of compassion, and to be too ready to understand all and forgive all; while Yves was in the trap for those inferiors who aspire to benefit from entering into relationships above their moral, cultural, emotional and even social stations, but cannot bear the pressure of being made to feel inadequate and second-rate and second-class. The history of such mismatches was stained with blood and tears, I regretted to inform her.

'I did try to soften the impact of my answers to her next questions. No, there was nothing to be done, for, as she herself had indicated, she would not get over her guilt if she left her husband. At least her situation would not change for the worse so long as she did not weaken: she must conserve her energy and hang on to her health – if she were to fall ill he would punish her for letting him down and never relent and harry her to her grave. Alternatively, supposing she was able to stick it out and survive him she would possibly be glad.

'I refrained from adding that Martine and Yves were the victims not so much of each other as of their own frailties. She must have searched for a man who would dominate her or try to, a replacement for her father, an instructor – she was still searching for him as she sat under my pine trees and implored me to help with her poetry and solve the riddle of her existence; and he needed a woman who would accommodate his sado-masochistic urges. I also omitted to give her a piece of unethical advice that was often on the tip of my tongue.

'She followed it telepathically nonetheless. One afternoon when the subject of her troubles was more or less exhausted, when our friendship had ripened in the dappled sunlight under the trees, and following a pause in which our trains of thought must have been positive, she remarked that she had much to be thankful for and was feeling a great deal better. I agreed with the first sentiment and congratulated her in respect of the second – and she corrected me. She was not talking about her marriage, except indirectly, but about the person who had rendered it endurable, a wonderful man, the secret mate of her body and her soul, for whose love she gave constant thanks to the good God.'

Adults and Adultery

I risked a cliché and said to Grace: 'I wish you were here.'

It was another perfect day. The cloudless sky was the pale blue of morning, and the sunshine bright without burning. I had walked down to Villefranche and round the bay and found a phonebox in the little square overlooking the *Port de la Santé*.

Grace followed my bad example and asked: 'Are you all right?'

'Are you?' I returned.

These two questions might be called the leitmotif of love.

We said in unison that we were sorry to have missed each other telephonically the previous morning.

'What was it like, your day out with Oliver?' I asked.

Tiring, she said, exhausting, and of course thankless.

'Was Nice nice?' she asked.

So much so, I replied, that I was determined to show her the *Baie des anges* and flower market one fine day.

'What's the score at the Villa Valerie?'

Doubtful – and indescribable, considering how complex everything was and the scarcity of my small change – my money would run out before I had told half the story. But, I continued, last night had been more peaceful than the night before, and to the best of my knowledge Gerbert was still in the land of the living.

I had to explain – Grace demanded explanation. I gave her an abbreviated account of the doctor's visit in the night before last, my fears of one sort and another, and Gerbert's punctual report for duty in the library as the teller of cautionary tales.

'Were we wrong to think he was the devil's disciple?' she inquired.

'I don't know – I've been wondering if he's on the side of the angels.'

'When he nearly died, or if he nearly died, were you sorry?'

'Yes and no – I would have been sorry not to know the end of the story.'

'Have you decided to write it all down?'

'That depends. It depends partly on you. I promised not to write another book.'

'Oh but I took your promise with a pinch of salt. I'm not the wife of a writer of fiction for nothing.'

I laughed and thanked and reminded her: 'But you haven't told me how you are.'

'Nor have you.'

We agreed that we might be worse although we were apart.

She then said: 'Crystal had a funny turn yesterday.'

'What sort of a turn?'

'She collapsed in the garden. Talking of death, I was afraid she was dead.'

'That doesn't sound funny.'

'She recovered quickly, and Tim West and the other vet both said she was good for her age and it was nothing to worry about.'

'What did they think it was?'

'Possibly a tiny fit.'

'I don't want her to have tiny fits.'

'Or she could just be pining for you.'

'You're joking.'

'Tim said it was another possibility.'

'Well, I'm worried even if he isn't.'

'Don't – she's perfectly healthy – she's at least as healthy as I am – and I'll probably have a fit if you don't come back to us soon.'

'My contract runs for tonight and two more nights – I'll be

home in four days – and I promise to hurry – please tell Crystal.'

At this point we were disconnected. As other people were queueing to use the phonebox, I vacated it and retraced my steps to Villefranche railway station. The ticket I bought was for Monte Carlo, and I waited for my train on a bench in the sun, trying to convey mental messages of comfort and cheer to my dear ones.

The train journey was sweet escapism – but what cannot be cured might as well be enjoyed. Tunnels through mountains alternated with stretches of line in a dazzle of sun beside the sea. We stopped at Beaulieu Mer, Eze Mer and Cap d'Ail, at sequestered platforms beneath palm trees with views of yacht basins, sleepy conurbations, schoolchildren in playgrounds and a lonely lighthouse. Dark green pines flourished in the rockiest soil and coloured the landscape. The frontier of Monaco was crossed and noticed by the greater number, height, newness and lavishness of the skyscrapers.

I walked up the hill from the station to the square with the casino on one side of it and the Hotel de Paris on the other. The traffic was solid and the cars seemed to be bigger and shinier than they were anywhere else. The hotel was guarded by daunting white marble steps, polished brass rails, a menu in a glass case listing imaginative food and prices, a haughty commissionaire and its reputation. The smart shops displayed goods for those whose prayers had been heard at the altars of Mammon across the way. The square had a hillside garden, terraced and manicured, and there was a more extensive garden with promenades and a free lift down to sea level behind the casino.

I took the lift and emerged on the road at the edge of the harbour where the better class of yacht was berthed – the marina was round the corner or over the hill on which stood the palace and the old-style residential area. Restaurants and cafés clustered here, some had tables and chairs on both sides of the road. Muzak featuring French accordions droned, and Japanese tourists took photographs of one another. The crowd and the atmosphere were cosmopolitan, but the prices were nationalistic – that is, affordable mainly by tax-free Monegasques.

I bought my lunch at a kiosk – a sandwich and some raisins on the branch – and walked to a quieter spot and sat on the harbour wall. The sea lapped behind me, the city soared up the mountainside in front, and I was able to spy on the activity on board the yachts moored in line fifteen or twenty yards from my vantage point. They were all crewed, they were large enough to need a professional crew and too valuable to be left unprotected. Obvious employees of both sexes with mariners' complexions mended and made good, polished and varnished. A few boats were ocean-going racers, sleek and tall-masted, their great sails furled. Most were motor-driven and had considerable superstructures boasting radio masts, radar apparatus, TV aerials and satellite dishes.

I munched my crusty sandwich filled with succulent cheese from Brie and looked across at the scrubbed hardwood deck in the stern of a yacht and into the saloon where a table was laid for lunch for eight or ten. It was really more of a small liner than a yacht, and luxurious rather than Bristol-fashion. I could see champagne bottles in an overgrown ice bucket, and now the owner, a short dark tubby man of indeterminate race wearing white shoes, white slacks with knife-edge creases, a double-breasted blue blazer with an excess of golden buttons and a white shirt open at the neck and showing the animalic black hair on his torso.

A car nosed along the road and stopped by the gangplank. A chauffeur jumped out and opened the rear door for a lady dressed in a charming grey outfit with a few yards of fur draped round her shoulders, and she and the yacht owner exchanged greetings in various languages and sociable kisses while the chauffeur unloaded matching luggage and a steward in white livery rushed to pick it up and carry it aboard.

I remembered that next week Mardi Gras would be celebrated – or was it the Monaco Grand Prix? I had noticed railed-off roadways and deduced that the yachts were being prepared for use, also that the hirsute plutocrat under observation was welcoming the first of the guests he had invited to see the fun and participate in the festivities. Another car came along and deposited four more guests, a mother and father and a couple of sixteen or seventeen-year-olds, a boy and a girl, beautifully dressed creatures with suntans that suggested recent skiing holidays in St Moritz or Aspen. Then a third car drew up and a couple of old sybarites, she with scanty hair as black as ink and legs like sticks, he in a loud check suit and an incongruous school cap embroidered with crossed oars, were helped across the gangplank.

The six elders and betters sat on deck-chairs, sipping champagne. Now the captain of the ship in pristine whites came to pay his respects to the company. Now a male secretary in a dark suit approached his boss with a whispered message and a mobile telephone. Somebody felt a draught: a rug was produced and wrapped round relevant knees. Somebody was suffering from the heat of the sun: an awning was immediately extended in order to provide shade. The young ones leant against the woodwork in elegant poses, holding icy glasses of indeterminate refreshment, looking bored and occasionally glancing at each other with a half-smile or a sneer. None of them showed awareness of the passers-by who stopped and stared, nor of myself on the harbour wall, which could be compared with a seat in the stalls.

The play I watched might be hackneyed, and the actors stereotypes. It and they were interesting nonetheless. They were actually of perennial interest to the whole wide world, as glossy magazines selling millions of copies attest. Wealth is more fun than poverty, whatever the do-gooders tell us. Wealth is another ideal, and to aspire either to have some or not to let others have more than you, to love or envy it or both, and to watch it in operation, are universal preoccupations.

Levellers are hypocrites. They draw the line between rich and poor to please themselves – the level they aim for is that which is most beneficial to themselves materially and socially. Besides, every organism has to hunt for its food, we have to hunt for the money with which to buy our food, and there is nothing necessarily wrong with those who are better hunters than most of us. Even the guests on the yacht had redeeming features, they were workers in the field of luxury and leisure. They had packed or organised their packing, donned their costumes, caught trains and planes to Monte Carlo, hired cars to transport them to the harbour, and were probably prepared to be civil to their host and his circle for the duration of their visit.

I reconsidered the younger generation, the plutocratic boy and girl. They seemed to be unimpressed by and unappreciative of their circumstances. They were apparently not pleased to be on a yacht worth millions in fabled Monte Carlo, and to have a golden future stretching ahead of them. They looked like a couple of casualties of excess, and paradoxically they reminded me of deprived youth, disaffected and rebelling against its lack of money and opportunities.

Would they ever be able to differentiate between pleasure and happiness? Do the rich have the patience, do the poor have the wherewithal, to seek love through thick and thin, without compromising, without reference to time? What chance did love have under pressure from wealth or poverty, therefore what would empty the concentration camps and leave the flowers to grow on the battlefields?

Those were the questions Gerbert was trying to answer, I reflected.

In the library the scene was the same – semi-darkness, the lamp on the desk with the wine, the girl in mute attendance, and my employer immobile behind his tinted spectacles and beard, struggling verbally to save his ideas from the clutches of death.

I asked if he was feeling better.

He answered with wit that old age enabled him to use the stock reply, 'Never better!', meaning in his case 'Always worse!', and that artists should not be given the chance to expatiate on the subject of their inevitable hypochondria.

He then launched into his monologue.

'Memory is man. If or when time robs us of our memories we shall be unrecognisable, the husks of what we once were, retaining only the power of ingestion and digestion. Without memory man becomes a machine.

'I stopped writing partly because I could no longer depend on mine, or was afraid that it might let me down. Every writer has reason to fear failure, the agony of the loss of confidence essential to the completion of a sentence, the agony of a book begun that cannot be ended and a contract and a heart broken. After all, as you know, and for better or worse, I can still string a few words together, and my second thoughts have flickered into the guise of inspiration. But my nights are haunted by the ghosts of forgetfulness. Once upon a time, when I wrote books, remembering dogged my waking and even my sleeping hours; now my concerns are that I have neither given enough practical advice nor issued enough warnings with sufficient force.

'If memory is man, art is energy: neither of those flashy statements tells the whole story, but, to generalise, a feeble old creative artist is a contradiction in terms. The companion with whom I'm sorry to say I spent last night was the worry that I had omitted to draw attention to the loveless ones, those who don't and can't love, the emotionally impotent who are so often too potent by half physically, for whom all the finer feelings are a closed book.

'I would not penalise success in order to encourage failure – not one crocodile tear shall be shed for people who lack metaphorical hearts. They are common but classless, dustmen as well as dukes, dunces and dons, soldiers and pacifists, and, although more rarely, females of all descriptions. They are apt to have bad backs to their heads – no bumps of sentiment – yet are keen to go through the motions of loving, and tend to marry often and to be promiscuous. They are not an edifying subject for discussion, and I would not waste my breath on them if they were not so dangerous and destructive.

'They may be innocent although guilty. They are impostors and frauds, but may never know why they maim and kill love. They are the reason to regret the passing of closed societies high and low in which everybody was acquainted with everybody else and youth knew roughly what to expect from its romances. They are another reason not to rush into intimate relationships, or sign on the dotted line of shared mortgage commitments with new lovers, or believe that brides and bridegrooms are all willing and able to keep their vows. They are why I would appeal to teachers and opinion-forming bodies to teach children not how sex is done, but what love can do, the cons and the pros.

'Yes, yes, I know – a counsel of perfection: but why bother to urge the world to settle for disappointment in love?

'I put the cons before pros in my ideal amorous syllabus. My memory is not so defective as to forget that youth needs no encouragement to join in the games that adults play. Moreover it was recently jogged by a short story I was sent by an aspiring writer labouring under the false impression that I still could, and would, help to get it published. The story was undoubtedly autobiographical and as sad as talentless work invariably is. Its hero is a married man in his later twenties, whose wife during her first pregnancy and after their baby is born will not grant him his so-called rights. She is a frail girl and fears for her health, and he sympathises with and loves her; but he is normal and strained to breaking point by chastity.

'The burden of the story is that the wife takes the baby to stay with her parents, and the husband is left alone in their home in London. He goes into the West End one evening and succeeds with difficulty in resisting the lures of prostitutes; but as he stalks the streets he passes a respectably dressed young woman and they exchange a glance of understanding. It is too late to accost her, he dare not turn back and catch her up, yet feels certain that she is starving for love and sick with sexual frustration as he is. He rounds a corner and sees her again in the distance and believes that he is seen, and begins an inner debate. He could pick her up, they could go somewhere, a park, a hotel, and relieve their feelings; but would it stop there, and could it become a terrible entanglement? Might he not be able to shake her off, might she be mad?

'She is standing outside a cinema, looking at the stills. He could so easily join her, he has either to walk past her or throw himself and his crying need, marriage, baby, life on her mercy, and now she is staring at and willing him to be brave and happy. He declines, he averts his eyes, he goes home, and soon the family is reunited. The twist is that he no longer desires his wife, he pines only for the unknown woman in the street, and eventually his marriage falls apart.

'Virility is so shy to start with, so diffident, and grows into such a bully. The hunger gnaws at our entrails and forces us to risk all for nothing much in the way of nourishment. We would sink our teeth in unclean meat and drink from the poisoned chalice.

'And sex is the instant matchmaker. And since sex can have nothing to do with compatibility, shared interests, mutually acceptable characteristics and longer term advantages, it falls back upon and fosters the catastrophic illusion that one person can mould and shape another to suit him or her.

'Enlightened self-interest of the materialistic sort is a solid basis for contentment at any rate. Most men want a cook-housekeeper and most women a child and a breadwinner, and the next best thing to love that doesn't count the cost is a bargain. But souls have to be satisfied too, and are apt to be pernickety and presumptuous. Setting aside ignorance, which accounts for the preponderance of universal wretchedness, and lack of education which accounts for another hefty percentage, attitudes that rebel against nature, including kindness carried to extremes, render many a promising partnership unworkable.

'Kindness and compassion are wonderful human faculties, but they stretch nature to the limit. We were never meant to be sorry for what we eat, we were designed to survive, not to weep exclusively over the pain and death of other beings. Kindness is wrong when it becomes suicidal, charity begins at home, caring is a luxury, priorities have to be kept in order.

'Pubescent girls should be given instruction in why to beware of pity. Women are kinder than men, and more adaptable and more reckless, and therefore more at risk. Martine, the wife of Yves, was convinced by his protestations that she could help him. She was persuaded that she alone might have the power to save him from some nasty undefined fate, and she hoped that he would help her in her loneliness and financial plight, and that she would be fulfilled by dedicating her life to such a good cause.

'But his idea of matrimony, as it turned out, was to provoke his wife until she slapped him down, and she found she could only keep their marriage on the rails by loving and being loved by another man.'

After supper Gerbert said: 'Marriage in its Christian form isn't easy. It's as difficult as loving your neighbour. But what's the point of aiming low? Alternatives to a monogamous intersexual linkage for life have never found favour in the western world.

'Although some young people may be against it nowadays, I remember a young friend of mine wailing "if only we'd married!" He had been living with a woman he wanted to get away from; he thought that if they had been married he could have divorced her in accordance with the laws of the land, whereas to leave her was to be confronted by a hundred and one personal moral dilemmas.

'Incidentally, the fashion not to marry was no doubt set by men. The feminists have made divorce too expensive for potential husbands, and achieved the unintended consequence of robbing potential wives of many a good husband and father for their children.

'If marriage seems to be the answer to long-term love, adultery often seems to be the answer to marriage. The word itself is suggestive: sophisticates say it's the adult thing to do. Cynical comments on the subject abound, for instance, "Nothing freshens up a marriage like a little adultery". Perhaps the operative word in that quote is the "little": some men and women can forgive and forget a slip, and the offenders can stop short before more damage is done. And then there are secrets that are kept, notwithstanding the truism that people in love always behave badly.

'Forbidden fruit has been tempting ever since it grew in the Garden of Eden. I've seen many fall for it, and have tasted it myself – one of the books I never wrote would have been called *The Omnibus of Adultery*. I'll describe a particular case, a representative example, more commonplace than Martine's. My claim to know the story from start to finish is supported by the fact that, despite the generation gap between us, I had been the best man of the lover.

'He was called Tony, and he married young. He was a country boy, son of a smallholder, a scion of yeoman stock, strong, red-cheeked, good-natured, generally slow, but quick at figures. He severed his connection with the land, and went to night school and qualified as a chartered accountant. His first job in accountancy took him to the homes of moneyed clients, in one of which he was introduced to the daughter of the house, a wilful only child, who fell in love with him. He was attractive to women, he looked so healthy and the brown curls on his forehead were reminiscent of a young bull, and he was not at all frightened of them and took them seriously.

'Sue was twenty-one and Tony twenty-six, and she made a dead-set at him. He was by no means averse and she was a pretty blonde and a catch by social standards. So they married in church with myself in attendance, bought a house in Battersea with a garden, had three children and seemed to be destined for happiness ever after.

'But fate does not approve of foregone conclusions. Tony was doing better and better, Sue was finding motherhood burdensome. Their garden was too small, the children's schools were too far away, and money was now available for a second home. They invested not in a cottage in Wiltshire, where they might have camped at weekends and for holidays, but in the sort of house she was accustomed to, with eight bedrooms, half an acre of garden, two paddocks and stabling. Tony was worried by the size and expense of the place; Sue reminded him that her capital would pay for a lot of the purchase price.

'I was their guest in Wiltshire on a number of occasions. They had both emerged from the amorphous state of youth, and their characters were defined together with the element of incompatibility in the marriage. They were both hospitable, but Sue made it clear to me that I was Tony's guest and friend. She was a sad example of the ravages that can be wrought on English complexions by time and the weather. Her pink and whiteness had turned rusty red, which imparted a peculiar coldness to the pale blue of her eyes. Her nose was sharper, her lips and her hair thinner, and she used cosmetics to ill effect; and her voice was louder than before. She and I had no interests in common – she never mentioned my books – and she ruled the roost at home in ways I found unattractive. She was easily annoyed by her husband and her children.

'He was unspoilt inasmuch as he was still quiet and unassuming, but whereas he had been uxorious, or at least relaxed in the company of his wife, he had now, as it were, installed shutters that could be closed against her. He yielded to her authority or authoritarianism, raised no objections, treated her coolly, and lavished affection on their issue. He was busy at weekends, playing cricket and tennis and indoor games of cards and hide-and-seek, teaching the youngest to ride a bicycle, taking the older ones to Pony Club shows, relieving Sue of parental chores and thus keeping his distance. On Sunday evenings he would drive me back to London and open up – I mean speak freely and with more spirit.

'They had sold the Battersea house and bought a small flat in Chelsea. It was all right for Tony, he just slept there and drank a cup of coffee for breakfast during the working week, but not for Sue. She felt cramped in it, poisoned by metropolitan fumes, at a loose end, and had pressing reasons to remain in the country, children's schooling, livestock to see to, the difficulty of finding dependable staff, the fear of burglary. Moreover she was not clever and she was complacent. She drove through the amber lights of matrimony, she seemed not to have heard of the mischief that unchained husbands can get into, she would not stoop to consider that Tony could be so common as to play her false, and was too dominant to think he would dare. She said she would spend Tuesday and Wednesday nights in London, and otherwise stay at home, that is in Wilts.

'One effect of her ruling was that I saw more of Tony. He asked me to dine with him on quite a few Mondays and Thursdays. He would speak loyally of Sue, explain that she could not stand London and he did not blame her; but I was left with the impression that he felt at once puzzled to be taken for granted and rather relieved. Then his secretary resigned. Miss Hicks had worked for and with him for a dozen or so years. She was a treasure, the old-fashioned type although only in her early ies, efficient, motherly. Tony depended on her, he said she was indispensable and did his best to dissuade her from looking after her aged relation exclusively, but she was adamant. His new secretary caused him headaches – she was called Clare.

'He complained of Clare to me – that she was a nice enough girl but a muddler and too easily upset. Time passed, maybe a year or two, and Tony rang up. He asked me round to his flat, not to dinner at his club, and that evening, that Monday or Thursday evening, instead of a week or two ahead. I went, I was curious to know why he had sounded agitated by his standards.

'Inevitably he and Clare had fallen in love. She was younger, prettier, kinder, gentler than Sue, and had been recovering from a broken engagement to marry another man, and they had consoled each other. The story was hackneyed, but he was not well versed in romance and was pleased to tell it. The affair started after a protracted day's work. They had been alone in his office in the big silent building at night, had brought the work in question to a successful conclusion, celebrated with a drink and one little kiss, which led to everything, including the exchange of vows of love everlasting. Clare made him happier than ever before, they were completely happy together in their world that was new and beautiful, and so on.

'His agitation was due to excitement mingled with guilt. It was probably first love for him and certainly his first difference of opinion with religion and morality. He was too decent to blame his wife for pushing him in an adulterous direction, and insisted that both he and Clare were determined not to injure Sue or his children – he could not get over Clare's unselfishness. He assured me that his marriage had suffered no losses and gained considerably from his improved state of mind as a result of the new situation. He was not worried about the future – it would take care of itself – Clare was such a good person – love would find a way.

'I cannot remember the time-scale of the vindication of my scepticism. Tony was no fickle and ruthless Don Juan, he was earnest and straightforward, a fit subject to be tied in knots by women, and Clare, however good, was sensitive and temperamental, and the habit of adultery has always been to start small and grow bigger. He either thought he could benefit from the experience of the writer of my fiction or used me as a sort of father-confessor, although I could only listen without absolving him. A series of telephone calls informed me that Clare required him not to share his marital bed with Sue at weekends; that Sue was hurt by his removal with his pillows to a spare room and sought to lure him back with unwonted offers of sex which he had to refuse; that he felt not only embarrassed but shamed by having to lie to Sue when she rang him early one morning and he was sleeping in Clare's flat; that his lies were multiplying and getting him down, for instance when he took Clare to a restaurant and they ran into one of Sue's friends, and again when he and Clare spent a weekend by the sea.

'Yes, he was incredibly happy whenever he had a chance; but the generalised message I received suggested that he was already lost in the maze of adultery. He invited me to meet Clare, we dined together in her flat. She had her attractions and was agreeable, but I could see she was wondering if I was on her side or on Sue's. I sensed her latent hostility and even her jealousy of my confidential friendship with Tony. I noticed her wincing whenever he referred to events in Wiltshire or his children, and saw signs of discontent with her lot. Her flat was cramped, she said, strictly for a bachelor girl – she longed for a house of her own but had never been able to afford one. Tony worked too hard, she said, ideally he should take the earliest retirement and return to his roots in the country, a cottage with an acre miles from anywhere – how they, how she, would love that!

'A secretarial mistress as easily upset as Clare was far worse than a mere secretary of similar disposition. She was sulky or made scenes after she had put Sue's telephone calls through to Tony, and devastated when one of his children wanted to speak to him. Another of his difficulties was that she now took it on herself to shield him from trouble at work – she opened and sometimes destroyed important letters addressed to him, and snapped at difficult clients that he was unavailable. His Christmas, Easter and Bank Holidays at home were ruined by his loyalties which Clare divided increasingly with the stiffness of her upper lip, with her tears, with her objections to being deserted, with her begging him to consider her for a change and charging him with not loving her truly.

'And his fair-mindedness did not permit him to force such issues. She was only trying to protect him in the office, he realised, and her unselfishness could not be expected to continue to yield him up willingly to a wife who cared nothing for his welfare. He had to pay the price for finding that, against the odds established by his staid personality, he had become the object of adoration and worship. Even without her hints and pinpricks he was painfully aware that the sacrifices were all on her side – she was missing her chances to marry and have children and be better off for his sake, she was an extra in his life whereas he was everything in hers – and that the least he could do to balance the books of their attachment was to make allowances and indulge her moods of justified frustration.

'He expressed wishes and hopes to calm her down if not exactly promises. And they still had wonderful times and told each other how happy they were. That their love was star-crossed lent it the authenticating touch of tragedy, and separation intensified it. Tony yearned, Tony suffered in the region of the heart for the first time in his life, and Clare insisted that he should shoulder some of the responsibility for, and sympathise with, her suffering. He became more soulful, read the books with which Clare comforted her solitude, even read poetry as well as his customary columns of figures, and developed a kind of idealism. In place of his ambition to succeed in worldly terms was a yearning to be alone with his mistress and to dedicate himself to her service.

'It was at this point in the old story that his wife discovered the telltale trace of infidelity on clothes she was washing for him; or maybe the stubs of theatre or cinema tickets or entries in his diary or a silly souvenir in the pocket of a coat she took to the cleaners gave the show away.'

Gerbert started to cough and I wondered if he would die. His head lolled and he coughed weakly behind a trembling white hand; but Marie rose and bent over him with her shapely white back to me, and must have again administered a pill or potion, for he stopped, she returned to her chair by the desk, he denied that he ought to rest, and said with a mixture of forcefulness and charm in his re-oiled voice: 'Forgive me! Listen, if you will! That more or less inevitable discovery is the crux of the matter for adulterers. Listen – somebody will win, somebody will lose – the injured party is about to pass sentence. Sue did not kick Tony out of the marital home and thereby sealed the fate of Clare.

'It took time to happen – I'm talking of years – and something else completed the process; but Sue, either from motives of affection or from malice, decided not to let her husband go – she would not play into the hands of her rival. She cursed him; aggravated his guilt; took a tough line – "Who is the whore? Good God, not your secretary! How corny can you get! Well, I'm not going to worry, I refuse to believe you'll wreck your life and your family for that vulgar sex-starved spinster!"; then subsided into the complaisant mode, offering cooperation on condition that he always told her where he was and – within limits – what he was doing.

'He agreed. He was relieved. A reasonably nice person cannot be nasty to someone who is being nice; and he thought he was lucky not to have to tell any more lies. But Sue was shrewd although not very clever: women do not need to be clever to defeat men in the war of the sexes. Tony now had to lie to Clare or at least not to reveal that he had told Sue they would be sleeping in the same bed on such-and-such a night. He did his best not to tell Clare that Sue had been understanding and was being sweet, and that the atmosphere in Wiltshire was improving out of recognition. But Clare suspected it, she wheedled enough of the truth out of him to know that she was done for, and was first angry, then sad..For Tony it was far more of a strain to be with her than it was to be with Sue, and there were no children to act as buffers between them.

'Everything was upside down. Not his fellow-adulterer but his spouse was his safety-valve and means of escape. Not Clare but Sue beckoned him towards a haven of repose and recuperation. He had broken his word of honour given in the house of God, stepped off the beaten track into bandit country, lived on his wits for the sake of his personal satisfaction, when nearly all for which he had put himself beyond the moral pale had been available in the legitimate security of his home. Was it an ideal he had aspired to, or was it greed that had driven him to make such a big mistake? The sadness of Clare was getting and only could get worse, and each of her tears seemed to turn into another link in the chains that bound him to her, while Sue's conduct, as intended and notwithstanding its beneficial effects, filled him with nostalgia for the good old days when his conscience was clear.

'They both appealed to me for guidance in this gathering storm – I mean Clare as well as Tony. She was too desperate to be wary of me, she thought she might be able to use me to influence her lover, she paid me a visit and poured out her sinking heart. She must have been forty-six by this time. She had dyed her blonde hair, which looked thin and dry, and her make-up was excessive and counter-productive – the mascara round her frightened eyes dated and aged her. She was foolish to show so much of her neck and chest, and her bare elbows were a disaster. She complained of the change in Tony, his new awkward temper, his unkindness, and enumerated the favours she had showered upon him. Her refrain boiled down to one pathetic question that begged a thousand others: "What have I done wrong?"

'Tony also sought me out. He was a shadow of his former self. The brown curls on his forehead had gone the way of all flesh, and his remaining hair was greyish. His complexion was more liverish than rubicund, and his steady slowness had been replaced by a jumpy sort of impatience. Of course his uninterrupted success in his work could have accounted for some of his physical disintegration. But his two questions were nothing to do with the financial type of accountancy. "Shall I ever be free?" he asked, and then: "How am I to redeem myself?"

'Fate answered him. Fate with the assistance of time can usually settle the impossible questions raised by adultery. Moreover the settlement is very often achieved by the single word descriptive of a particular fact of life. That word is "illness".

'Eternal triangles are held together by health. The moment one of the three parties involved is ill, seriously sick, the triangle collapses. Illness is more pressure than the pressurised structure of adultery can bear.

'If Tony had been the ill one, Clare who had no rights would have been cast into outer darkness – Sue and the practicalities of nursing him would have denied her access to the bedside. Again, if it had been Clare, Tony might well have left Sue in order to look after her, he would have blamed himself and remembered that she was the love of his life and regarded his action in the light of redemption. But Sue had the bad or good luck to contract the disease in question; and amongst her advantages in the context of adultery's tug-of-love were her wedding ring, her offspring, the marital home she presided over, and the solution she was providing to the problem of Tony's loyalties, to wit an excuse to detach himself from the accomplice of his wrongdoing.

'He bade Clare farewell, or, as he hypocritically put it or tried to, goodbye for the time being.

'His marriage profited in the short term. He was glad to be back on the straight and narrow, and Sue was obviously glad not to have to think of Clare hovering like a vulture in the background. But Sue did not die. She recovered and ascribed her close shave to the strains of his unfaithfulness, and, sure that he had learnt his lesson and was hers for ever, began to punish him for all he had put her through. And Tony was nagged by new regrets and by chronic remorse. He had stolen Clare's best years, robbed her of her womanly opportunities, led her up the garden path and betrayed her. He yearned in vain to try to make reparations, but she had disappeared, had been careful not to let him know where she was, and anyway he could not have borne to re-encounter her rage, her accusations, her contempt and her wretchedness.

'Tony spoke to me for a last time. His life was luxurious on the outside, he said, and dust and ashes within. I was rather glad not to hear from him again. As one grows older one has less liking for stories with unhappy endings.'

Inordinate Affection

We told each other we were well and I asked how Crystal was.

I had walked to Villefranche through another blue and silver morning and was speaking to Grace from one of the telephone boxes on the little square.

Grace said: 'She's okay, she seems to have recovered completely.'

'What sort of a fit did the vet think it was?'

'He wasn't sure – he's only known Crystal since we moved down here. Dogs have funny turns for hundreds of different reasons apparently.'

'You saw Tim West, didn't you, not another of the vets in the practice?'

'Yes.'

'What was the prognosis?'

'Roughly speaking "don't worry" – but he wasn't too happy about her heart.'

'What's wrong with her heart, for pity's sake?'

'I don't know – he said it's not life-threatening.'

'Cold comfort! What's he going to do about it?'

'Not a lot, he doesn't want to upset the dog's constitution. She's herself again, and the risks are slight, and he'd rather hold the pills in reserve for when she needs them more than she does at present.'

'We mustn't let her die.'

Grace laughed at me and said: 'She isn't on her death-bed or in her death-basket yet. I guessed you'd take the news too much to heart, and thought it could wait until you were here with us, but for some reason I can't keep a secret from you. Isn't that what every husband hopes to hear? I promise it won't be my fault if she decides to swap rude good health for kicking the bucket in the next forty-eight hours. There hasn't been a change of plan, has there – you will be back the day after tomorrow?'

'Definitely, all things being equal.'

'Thank the Lord! But why the qualification?'

'I thought Gerbert was a goner yesterday evening. He was discussing adultery, and it nearly polished him off.'

'Not surprising at his age.'

'His cautionary tales aren't personal, they're more like case histories. Anyway, Marie stopped him coughing somehow, although the doctor was again at the villa half an hour ago. Docteur Palin and Monsieur Kolnatsch, and the physio and a new starchy nurse were all in attendance – the whole gang was hard at it for a price. Who's paying, I can't help wondering, where's the money coming from? Can Gerbert be that rich? Is her bountiful ladyship signing the cheques? Time will tell – not enough time to go into it now. He's determined to do his survey of love or whatever it is. If his determination doesn't carry him through, I'll be home sooner.'

'Well – such an ill wind would be good for me, although I shouldn't say so.'

'Ditto. How's Oliver? Sorry, I ought to have asked after Oliver first.'

'Physically he's not bad, socially he's not good. He's more of a curmudgeon than ever – yesterday I told him he ought to write his biography and call it *How to be your own worst enemy*. But he's leaving soon, and then I'll be sorry I haven't been nicer to him. He knows how awkward he can be, he says he'd better make himself scarce before you return.'

'Poor old Oliver! Poor rich Gerbert – I pity him provided there's ten thousand to spare for me! Poor Crystal! We seem to have strayed into the front line, don't we?'

'Oh we're always in that, but let's look on the bright side. Is my sun shining on you?'

We exchanged meteorological information in accordance with Anglo-Saxon practice, and as usual wished we were together. Our more intimate conversation was cut short by impatient tourists rapping on the glass side of the telephone box.

My plan was to take the minibus to the top of the hill, or rather the so-called mountain, and walk down. I had noticed that such a bus service was available, and was sure the views would be splendid and the houses interesting up there. It was now about eleven-thirty, and the sun which also shone on Grace cast temperate beams out of an unblemished sky. I crossed the road to the bus stop and, after reading the time-table and realising I had a quarter of an hour in hand, returned to the square and mounted one of the flights of steps to the old-style alley where the four shops were located and the air was permanently scented by the delectable aroma of baking bread. In the best of bakeries, where cakes beyond the dreams of gluttony were also made, I bought my lunch of a sandwich filled with butter and ham, and in another shop a couple of oranges.

I had one fellow-traveller in the bus, a Frenchman, an unshaven pensioner wearing a beret and not taking kindly to the vicissitudes of the road. The hairpin bends that we began to round with unnecessary flair called forth his criticism of our driver, of the drivers of the vehicles we narrowly missed, of the transportation policies of his government and the bitterness of existence. Notwithstanding his forecasts of disaster we were soon safely above the red roofs and TV aerials of the houses of the *vieille ville*.

Houses, villas large and small, formed a sort of vertical ribbon development on the hillside. They either had been or would be built on every scrap of land that could be levelled, or allowed for terraced constructions, or was suitable for developments on stilts; and cars were parked on the edges of precipices. Here and there the terrain was too steep even for the resolute ingenuity of the local builders, and sheer walls of rock seemed to threaten to fall on the bus or to push it into the oncoming traffic. But our driver was intrepid, to give him the benefit of the doubt, and at various scheduled stops other travellers entrusted themselves to his skill.

The whole journey was due to take twenty minutes. After fifteen, I was again alone with the tetchy OAP until we picked up a lady with a springer spaniel. The lady was a regular customer on the bus, I gathered, and was taking it to where she could give the spaniel his morning walk. He was in a great state of excitement, wagging his tail, panting, barking, and then involved in a scene of recognition. The man in the beret held out a hand that was all knobs and veins, and when the dog rushed to lick it his face assumed expressions of pleasure, he smiled and showed a tooth or two, patted and stroked the dog's head with his free hand, mumbled terms of endearment, and in short was mollified and transformed. The lady apologised and laughed with typical Latin sprightliness, the dog's friend signalled that for once he had no complaints, and I thought of Crystal and we arrived at our destination.

We were at the *Place St Michel*, a vantage point and car parking space somewhat below the summit of the particular *Alpe Maritime* that cradles the bay of Villefranche. The lady with her springing spaniel bustled off in the direction of a treed area, and the beret disappeared down a steep path. The bus driver pointed out my way as indicated on my map, and we said *au revoir*.

It was breezier here. In days gone by no one lived beside the sea if they could afford to live as high as possible above it: they considered sea air unhealthy, and knew they would be cooler in summer in and on the hills. The view was endless over the descending shelves of houses and the trunk roads – between the promontories of Mont Boron and Cap Ferrat – across the sea where the Villefranche fishing boats cast their nets and into a haze of distance that lent additional mystery to the planetary curve. I resisted the temptation to lighten the load in my pockets by eating it, and began to walk back to the Villa Valerie.

A lane zigzagged under pine trees filtering the sun. Crickets sawed and chirruped, and tiny birds, so small as not to be caught and eaten by the natives, squeaked and flitted in the topmost branches. The breeze had subsided or else I was sheltered from it, and the brooding silence seemed to be deepened by the muted sounds of civilisation, internal combustion engines and pile-drivers at work. Every so often one dog barked and others joined in, and the canine chorus ended reminiscently with a few snarls and whines.

The architecture I stopped to study took some getting used to. The point of it was clearly to admit the maximum amount of sun and scenery into the houses at all costs. Northern elevations might have been designed for prisons, whereas the windows facing south were picture and plate-glass and angled without regard to symmetry, and balconies were thrown out with abandon. A lot of the houses were unoccupied, second homes probably reserved for odd weekends and summer holidays, and old-fashioned indoor and outdoor shutters and new-fangled metal screens were reinforced by the notices on garden gates bearing the legend: *Chien méchant*. Common proofs of habitation were accordion music on the radio or the housewife in bedroom slippers beating a carpet on a balcony, and *chiens* more or less *méchants* at garden gates. The poodles were surely inclined to be philanthropic, but the huskies and big mongrels conscientiously showed me their teeth.

But to revert to the architecture, it might be undistinguished, it nonetheless had the charm of purposefulness and practicality, and the rougher edges were smoothed by paint in strong Mediterranean colours and the bougainvillea climbing everywhere. Moreover the French genius for making do imparted a homely touch to older properties – a rickety awning of corrugated iron, blue geraniums growing in halved car tyres ranged round a lily pool. And then of course the magic of the sun had the power to turn ugliness into beauty, or almost to do so, and the lush strong green of pines and cypresses, the subtle green of olive trees, the green sprouts in vegetable patches, the riot of verdancy anticipating spring was like a flattering veil drawn across the face of the landscape.

Walking downhill is hard on unaccustomed legs, and after half an hour of it I reached and rested on a seat in a sort of arbour. I was above and some twenty-five yards from one of the *corniches*, too close to the traffic for comfort; on the other hand I could look over the cars at the parkland of La Leopolda, the stately home built by the King Leopold of the Belgians who had tried and failed to acquire the site of the Ephrussi-Rothschild villa. Better still, I could eat my lunch.

The slopes of the park in front of me betrayed the fact that money had been lavished on them, money mainly in the form of water – they were greener than nature intended. The estate had changed hands recently, another wealthy cosmopolitan had bought it, and as always the evidence that talent had been able to assert itself in spite of egalitarians, socialists, envy and spite was a source of satisfaction and encouragement. In every sphere of existence, including love as Gerbert was in the process of arguing, there was one law for those who can't and won't and don't, and another for those who play for high stakes and occasionally win.

I did not arrive at that somewhat platitudinous conclusion by referring particularly to Gerbert. Ever since resolving that I might try to write an account of his valedictory discourses, I had obeyed the literary rule of neither talking about nor even thinking of the joint work possibly in progress: writers worth their salt learn to let their subconscious minds supervise most of the act of creation. But I now spared a thought for his losers, for the unloving and unloved, for the unsuccessful unhappy majority.

I laid down my sandwich and remembered Grace's remark that we were all in the front line. Although it did not altogether take away my appetite, I suffered an awful pang of my fear of the future and of fortune, to which I had given the most precious of hostages.

We were back in the library, and I urged him to take a night off, not to hold forth for hours on end. Even in the discreet lighting and notwithstanding his dark glasses he looked bloodless and wasted, and his straight back had bent and he was more slumped in his chair.

'Couldn't it all wait till tomorrow?'

He replied with the shadow of a smile: 'I'm not so optimistic as that.'

He then began: 'Marriage is unfashionable and for the moment unpopular. Marriage is in decline and out of date, they say. The restless remember how long it can be, the ruthless thank heaven it can be short. Men count the cost for better or worse. Poor women have no defence against husbands, and rich ones see a fortune-hunter in every pair of trousers. Both sexes dread the responsibilities they may be incurring at the altar: a spouse with criminal inclinations, a filthy temper, expensive tastes, ailing health. Maternal types are never certain that their bridegrooms will prove to be good fathers; and every woman weakened and hampered by childbearing wonders if her husband is going to abandon her and their offspring.

'Matrimonial misery can be great on account of reasons that seem small to outsiders. One partner's unpunctuality, facial tic, catchphrases or clumsiness can drive the other partner to drink or the divorce court. Minor irritations become major owing to the permanency or idea of the permanency of the marital tie – a life sentence according to the Christian religion. Moreover husbands have been known to be cruel, wives to hen-peck, and both to be unfaithful. Most husbands are stronger than and capable of beating their wives, while most wives are shrewder and have better nervous systems than their husbands, therefore win the arguments. Bruises and broken bones are the lot of many wives; sexual frustration and humiliation destroy the peace of mind and the confidence of husbands. Marriage can easily spell the death of the heart, the death of hope and ruin in the material sense.

'Wedding bells do not guarantee joy. Books that conclude with marriage do not necessarily have happy endings. Read the gutter press which revels in the blood and tears of domestic scenes, before you agree to sacrifice your self-reliance and your freedom!

'Yes, but what's the alternative?

'Without a formal promise of support and a degree of security who will bear your children? Where will you go for sex if not to the partner who has promised to provide it? Who will keep solitude at bay? Who has said he or she will look after you when you're ill, and close your eyes for the last time?

'Institutionalised monogamy may be an ideal that's never attained, but polygamy must be more difficult. It's not only unthinkable for emancipated western women, and for women anywhere who are naturally inclined to be competitive, proprietorial, jealous and to hate a successful sister, but impossible without duress. All societies dominated by men and founded on the principle that might is right are bad for women by modern standards. Equally, the right of either spouse to put aside a better half, marry again and start another family, always leaves one of the two parties injured.

'The governance of sex in different societies isn't my pigeon. But how could any society be governed without the conventional or legal control of parenthood and protection of children? Everybody who knows anything knows that anarchy is the worst of all political evils.

'I wasn't a good father, but belatedly I would make restitution by speaking out against abortion on demand, and by recommending marriage and making divorce more difficult. Certainly widows have done wonders with the issue they are left to rear alone: and the mothers of accidental babies whose fathers disown them and disappear are often devoted and dutiful; but surely such upbringings, however well-intentioned, would be classed as second best by idealists and, with hindsight, by the children involved. And I believe a majority of children would vote against divorce even if they were having a horrible time at home.

'No, I don't underestimate the sufferings of the young who are tortured sexually and otherwise by parents. But the evidence suggests that a majority of children would prefer not to be fatherless or sired by a test tube, not to discover he or she is different, and not to have to come to terms with divided loyalties, with step-fathers or their mother's lovers, and all the hurtful compromises of divorce.

'Again, I'm not proud of my own matrimonial record. Truthfully, without false modesty, I'm proud of nothing except, as I began by telling you, that I've succeeded at last in not being the man I used to be. Here are my apologies for telling people to do as I say and not to do as I've done.'

After supper Gerbert told the following story.

'Toby was the grandson of a butler. He was a friend of my aristocratic friend Caroline. English society is classless, although the have-nots argue otherwise. All you have to do to ascend from the bottom of the social pile to the top is to make some money.

'Jesus said "The poor ye have always with you". I think He was misreported, He was too wise not to have added "and the same applies to the rich". Revolutions only remove one bunch of the loved and envied in order to replace it instantly with another. But that's beside the point.

'Toby's father was given a good education by the butler. He was clever enough to become a doctor and handsome enough to develop a fashionable practice in Harley Street. His second son Toby was reared in gentlemanly circumstances, and grew to look and to act the corresponding part. He was staying with Caroline when she introduced us: she was not a snob and did not differentiate between her breeding and his, or between hers and mine for that matter. She thought in her ingenuous way that he'd turn into a great writer. He visited me here, and we met a few times in England.

'He was twenty-something when we met, and I was about three times his age. He was charming, and he treated me with deference. His appearance was golden, he was a golden boy and a delight for the eyes and even a mirror of fashion – he fitted all those descriptions, and showed not a trace of his plebeian origins. He exuded health and confidence, and he seemed to have the character of good physical specimens, sweet rather than bitter, extroverted, straightforward.

'The question of literary talent remained. He had read a good few books and spoke glowingly about them, and about authors, art, work and getting down to it. But he shed a similar glow on his social life and his girlfriends. He had received exciting invitations, he was rushed off his feet by his friends, he was spoilt for choice by girls – he was an out and out heterosexual and probably a flirt, a Cherubino in the English mould with a fair complexion and freckles. Where did he, where would he, find the time for literary composition? The examples of his writing that eventually came my way were the opposite of everything he appeared to be – in a word they were dim.

'The content was derivative, the prose laboured and cautious. Juvenilia, published posthumously for some rotten reason, must have caused many a writer to turn in his or her grave. Excellent writers have produced reams of worthless and unworthy stuff to start with, especially if they have a poetic weakness for the sound of a sentence. Toby's first steps were faltering, but I had a vague inkling that he might have a book in him and write it when he stopped philandering and renounced prodigality. He was or said he was keen to learn. He referred to literature as if it were the holy grail.

'But I learned more from him than he did from me. I learned the inside story of his love affairs, whereas my professionalism, my discussion of grammar and which dictionary he should use, passed over his golden head or under his flying heels. He was the slave of his susceptibility – he was the new boy in the sweetshop of female favours, gorging himself at one moment, afflicted by romantic indigestion the next. He was worried by being called fickle by the girls he had kissed only once or twice. He was innocent, he claimed; it had not been like that, he protested. He indicated incoherently that he was trying to choose and decide. In other words, from my point of view, he was never a completely lost cause, while, perhaps from his, I was a sort of buoy to cling to so as to keep his head above the bubbly tide.

'Then he began to mention Miriam. He said he was intrigued by and attracted to a girl unlike others, and asked if he could introduce her to me. I agreed, although loath to be burdened by responsibility in such a personal matter. They were an ill-assorted pair, judging by appearances: he tall, willowy, lustrous, she short and very dark, with wiry black hair and large black eyes under strong eyebrows. She was not pretty, and she looked older or at any rate more mature than he was; but her strong features, individual style of dressing, composure and assurance were striking, and she was possessed of that aid to seduction which is no longer in vogue, beautiful elocution.

'They had none of the outward similarities that are supposed to cement a relationship; yet they might have been emotionally as well as physically complementary. He was light as air, and she looked as if she could bring him down to earth and tether him there. However, for the time being, she was playing his game, laughing at his jokes, following his lead, lending tacit support to his literary leanings, clearly loving him without reservations. What had I thought of her, he asked on a later occasion? I gave my blessing if not exactly my opinion. Well, he said, he was taking the plunge, probably making a mistake but not an irreversible one thanks to the divorce laws, he was fed up with fooling around and realised the party was over, and had picked on a girl who would be good to and for him, he hoped.

'Those were his inauspicious arguments for marrying. At least there were no money worries – he had modest private means and she was financially independent. They had lived in London for a year or two without producing children when Toby told me they were moving into the country. He agreed with Miriam that his writing would have a better chance if they were out of range of nonstop festivities. They bought a cottage in the back of beyond in Wales, and he wrote me letters which were full of books, books read, a development possibly better than nothing.

'Before too long my door was knocked upon as half-expected and I was assailed by his predictable outpouring. It was no use, he was not cut out for country life, he was unaccustomed to the deadly quietness and the boredom, and was going to call it a day.

'Yes, Miriam had been keeping his nose to the literary grindstone, and he hated that too, he was sick of writing and trying in vain to write, of solitude, rejection slips and feeling a failure. Miriam's confidence in him was misplaced, he said, and an additional strain – she was a better person than he deserved, for he found it difficult to live up to her standards. Anyhow the whole business of being a husband got him down, fidelity never had been and was not his forte – he was going to have to rethink his future and theirs. His catalogue of complaints was superfluous, because they were uncharacteristic, because he was pallid and fretful, not so much a happily married young husband as a lost soul heading for the law courts, and because the majority of potential divorcees say the same things.

'A year or two elapsed, and he called on me again. He looked better, but had a worse instalment of his story to tell. Miriam had had a miscarriage and lost their baby.

'It had happened some months ago – she had not yet recovered fully. I sympathised. I asked where they were now living. In the same place in the country, he replied – it was best for Miriam and he had grown fonder of it. What about his writing? Oh that, he laughed without any intonation of regret – he had no time to write, he was nurse, cook, housekeeper, gardener and chauffeur rolled into one, and glad to have such satisfying gratifying tasks since Miriam was on the mend. He was in London only for the day, and in order to make various purchases on her behalf.

'I was tactless, I was sorry he had settled for life instead of art, I harked back to his writing and to his confessions when we were last together and meant to encourage him by making the point that not having the welfare of a child to consider, not having a pram parked between himself and his desk, would give him greater freedom to follow his star and do what he pleased.

'He was shocked – or should I say aggrieved? His eyes filled with tears and he corrected me gently. He blamed himself for not explaining that he had acted on his former disloyal feelings. He had left home and run off with another woman, as a result Miriam miscarried, and he had the death of their baby on his conscience. No, he had not known about the pregnancy – Miriam's superstition was that it would have been tempting providence to break the news too early on. Of course, naturally, he had hurried back to her, and he would not stray again. Her forgiveness, the generosity of her love, were extraordinary and inspirational.'

'A short story's meant to have a surprising twist at the end; but the story I'm telling had several.

'I called at the cottage in Wales two or three years later, and had a private word with Toby and with Miriam in turn. It was teatime, and he went to cut the sandwiches and fetch the teapot, leaving me alone with her. Her eyes were deep and dark and she spoke well, but she was a dumpy creature, physically undistinguished, and a trifle complacent, even comparable to the cat that swallowed the canary. She said it was a pity that Toby never did any writing: why was it, what did I think? I duly supplied the demand, replying that he looked better than I had ever seen him, and the writing would have to wait. She was vaguely grateful. He was the sweetest man and she was the luckiest woman, she added.

'Toby and I talked when he showed me his vegetable patch. He said he was proud of his garden and its produce, and houseproud too – he had redecorated some of the rooms and repainted an exterior wall. He adored his wife, he confessed, and their marriage now meant everything to him – all the divisions were unified and the doubts dispelled. He omitted to mention his literary interests, let alone mine. Happiness is egoistic, and marriages that work create a world of their own and no one else's. They stood together at their garden gate, waving me away. He had been domesticated, and his fugitive talents rerouted into uxoriousness. My next reflection was that the women who are obsessively loved are seldom the beauties.

'The third was my sudden suspicion that Miriam was never pregnant and that the miscarriage was an imaginative means to the end of recapturing her errant spouse.

'But Miriam died. I record her death not callously but in short, so as to move ahead to its effect on Toby. I scarcely knew her and cannot pretend to be sad.

'In reply to my letter of condolence, Toby wrote that he

would never get over his loss. The phrase was hackneyed, but he meant it. For not knowing her heart was weak he blamed himself again. He wrote more letters in the following year or two. Miriam was irreplaceable, he declared repeatedly. There had been, was and could be nobody like her – and he enumerated her qualities and virtues. He celebrated their marriage as he had denigrated it not all that long before. He swore that he would never have tired of Miriam, forgetting that he had fled her in the fairly recent past. He was brainwashed, his memory was obstinately selective, he mourned with the energy and absorption he had previously brought to bear on flirting, getting married and trying to get divorced. No amount of misery, no self-mutilation, was enough to prove how much he loved and missed his Miriam. He almost gloried in the weight he had lost, the length of his uncut and unwashed hair, the commotion he caused in the supermarket, the embarrassment of acquaintances who threw him a word of sympathy and were caught in a shower of his tears.

'I was relieved not to meet him at this period, and dreaded his offer to pay me a visit. But he kept his distance, and his introspective epistles were at once a safety valve and a recrudescence of his yearning to be a writer. His sorrows were the source of fancies worthy of Edgar Allan Poe. He described his fits of anger with Miriam for having deserted him. He was frightened by nightmares in which he murdered her by stabbing and suffocation. He was racked by speculation that he had actually been the death of her, had suffered a blackout, gone mad, killed her, and had no recollection of his crime. He was haunted by her, sure that he had heard her voice mingling with the songs of birds in the garden, convinced that she had made love to him in their double bed one night.

'Eventually I protested. It was time to let the dead bury the dead and think about a new beginning. I resorted to clichés: he was not the only widower in the world – dear ones were dying every second of every minute of every day somewhere or other – he was too young to surrender unconditionally to grief – he must forgive me for reminding him that there were as good fish in the sea, and so on. I informed him that it had been and would be Miriam's wish that he should return to his writing. I also invoked his ancestry: he had come up in the world and must not sink down into decadence – it was too soon for a member of his family to settle for being effete.

'His reply was short and sharp: I did not understand. The point is arguable. My interference was effective in the short term inasmuch as it spared me further anguished letters, also in a limited literary sense. But I suppose I shouldn't take credit for the slim volume he wrote in the next five or six months, the period which culminated in his suicide.

'At his funeral the consensus of opinion was that Toby's end was tragic. But it was nothing of the sort – it was at best pathetic and at worst sinful. I have no patience with the romanticism of the nineteenth century, which held that death was preferable to life – healthy vigorous life – without the love of one beloved person. Toby's romanticism was out of date and more sulky than reasonable. He rejected the gift of existence. He believed this world had nothing more to offer him. He thought he knew better than fate. And I think he was wrong.

'In the graveyard a short woman standing on the other side of the open grave was the image of Miriam. She was crying discreetly and had thrown back her veil to press a handkerchief to her face. She had exactly the same strong eyebrows and large soft impenetrable black eyes. Scepticism was suspended – I thought she was a ghost. But after Toby was consigned to the dust she approached me and introduced herself. She was Miriam's sister, and the likeness was uncanny. Her harmonious vowels and consonants were identical.

'For some reason I liked her better than Miriam. She seemed more trustworthy, and she was more communicative. Toby had never mentioned her to me, but apparently she had looked after him since he was on his own. She had loved him, she said, she would have done anything for him – why had he thrown himself away?

'She sent me the typescript of his book. It had been rejected by various publishers, and she wondered if I could help to get it into print. Its title was *No Dominion,* a quote from the poem by Dylan Thomas that opposes and denies death. But death dominated throughout. The story or theme was that by taking his life the author would be reunited with his wife. The Christian religion was therefore travestied, and realism and common sense were conspicuously absent.

'However, before I had finished my reading, Miriam's sister conveyed the news that a reputable publisher had accepted the book after all. He liked and admired it, she told me, which I took to mean that he saw its commercial possibilities; and he had given assurances, which I disbelieved, that he was not influenced by the suicide, of which he would refrain from undue use for publicity purposes.

'My cynicism was not too wide of the mark. Morbidity helped the publisher to recover his costs. But, setting aside the influence of sensational journalism, his admiration was not misplaced, for the book was a respectable contribution to the literature of fantasy, and earned worthwhile praise as well as its costs. It would have made a sound foundation for Toby's future career as a writer. He could have realised his youthful ambition, and married a second wife physically indistinguishable from his first and perhaps superior in character.'

Love and Death

I made my morning call to Grace from St Jean Cap Ferrat, from *L'Elisir d'Amore*, the bar so suitably named considering whom I had been talking to and what had been talked about for the last five nights.

John of St John, archetypal French barman, shirtsleeves rolled above his elbows and short white apron encircling his hips, was serving alcoholic breakfasts at the farther end of the bar while I spoke in muted accents into the telephone at the other end.

Grace and I having assured each other we were all right, she told me Crystal was still better and I told her Gerbert was worse.

'What's happened?' she asked.

'His doctor arrived at the Villa with a nurse in full fig a couple of hours ago, and as I was leaving the premises his solicitor hurried in.'

'Where's her ladyship?'

'Ask me another!'

'Shouldn't she be rallying round the bed of sickness? You can't postpone your visit to an eighty-year-old who's feeling under the weather. What does Monsieur Kolsnatsch say?'

'He's called Kolnatsch, and he doesn't say much. He answers my questions by shrugging his shoulders, and the servants say nothing.'

'She can't love him.'

'Well, he loves her – I've received the impression or jumped to the conclusion that they worship each other. I hope he's okay, he's won me over, he's gallant and lucid and dares to say unfashionable things – and I was expecting this evening's session to reveal all. I'm longing to come home, but would have liked to hear his summing-up, what I suppose one would have to call his last words on the subject. Unfinished symphonies are a bit sad. On the other hand I may be with you sooner than planned.'

'Well, I won't say what I'm thinking.'

'Tomorrow I'll take my money and run – aeroplanes have seats available so early in the year – and if I can't get to a telephone in France I'll ring you when I touch down in England. You won't worry, will you?'

'Of course not, I never do,' she claimed with flattering irony.

'In twenty-four hours, thirty-six at the most, we'll be together again, please God.'

'Please, God, please me!'

'How's Oliver?'

'I'm driving him home tomorrow morning, so you won't be able to reach me between nine-thirty and midday. He's incorrigible, he's certain he can manage in his hermitage, crutches and solitude and isolation and old age notwithstanding. He was quite sweet to me yesterday evening, and grateful too, but he isn't happy. Nor am I temporarily, if it comes to that. But I can't say more for the moment. By the way, I think I may never let you out of my sight again.'

'Ditto!'

'Where are you?'

'In a bar with other people.'

'Drinking? Drinking at this hour?'

'Not yet, only trying to talk and not be overheard.'

'What next! I mean what are you going to do next, before you report back to headquarters?'

I explained, and the volume of noise in the bar increased, each of us was trying to tell the other that we were inaudible, and we had to ring off.

I said *au revoir* to John or Jean, and retraced my steps in the direction of Villefranche, therefore passing the gates of the Villa

Valerie and noting the black cars still parked behind the baobab and in front of the house: the crisis within must be unresolved.

But out of doors, by the sea, the crystalline air and unblemished blue sky seemed to counteract or postpone care. I strolled round the bay, where families were already encamped on the sandy strip and children shrieked and frolicked in the chilly wavelets. The omens were good at least for the local Festival of Flowers which was due to take place in the early afternoon.

My plan was to watch it: I had explained to Grace that with any luck the Festival in Villefranche was what would happen next. Advertisements for the show, which differed from others in the region in that it was seaborne, had been stuck in shop windows and had caught my eye. Already, at eleven o'clock or thereabouts, new maritime activities were in progress on the fishing boats in the little harbour. The fishermen were fixing shapes of wire mesh wherever possible and attaching flowers to them, while motorboats were roaring round with floral reinforcements from the other port and marina, the *Port de la Darse* behind the cliff that supported the remains of the *Citadelle*.

I had never seen the other port with its *darse* or wet dock for repairing boats, and now had time to investigate. A narrow rough path or promenade was cut out of the face of the cliff – I wandered along it as the sea broke against and washed the rocks a few feet below. Men and boys were fishing in the sun-shot depths, balancing on the slippery seaweed on minor promontories. The marina was chock-full of lines of boats of all sorts and sizes, from dinghies to yachts with swaying masts to monstrous motor cruisers, and beyond was the dock or boat-yard. Vessels again of every description were being worked upon both in and out of the water, one having its superstructure painted, another having its bottom scraped, and in nearby sheds carpenters sawed and blacksmiths hammered on anvils.

I sat on a seat in the shade cast by a plane tree and observed the varied activity. Here again fishermen were decorating their boats with flowers, especially mimosa – trucks and vans were dumping loads of yellow and green branches on the quayside. Wives and daughters helped husbands and fathers to weave sprays into the wire mesh, concentrating on the task, talking and laughing in lowered voices. In a strip of garden mothers gathered to gossip and rock prams, while toddlers fell over and crashed their pedal cars. Owners of the leisure craft were not much in evidence – I had scarcely seen a boat sailing or cruising since I had been in the South of France – perhaps life afloat was not the done thing at this time of year; but a few engines had been started to charge batteries and activate pumps, and the face of an occasional salt peered up and out from an open hatch, like that of a dog from its kennel.

The steady background noise was the tap-tapping against masts of ropes made of hemp or nylon – or were they metal wires? They used to be called sheets for some unknown reason, those ropes controlling sails, and the metal version was known as a shroud. I was reminded of Gerbert. Grace was right: where was his wife? He dwelt in the house called after her, he made a tract for the times of their marriage, and she was abandoning him in his hour of need to a speechless Indonesian girl and her family and to unsupervised men, doctors and lawyers probably on the make, bearing sinister black bags and driving hearse-like cars.

Writers resemble gardeners in at least one respect: they learn not to dig up a potential flower to check the state of its roots. I had not probed or pried into any of the French experience that I hoped to write about – I trusted it would grow into a satisfactory form on the page. But I was threatened with the loss of my last chapter, which is apt to be the best in a good book – and indeed a test of a book's goodness. If Gerbert expired I would not only be left with a literary fragment, I would also never know why Mr Curry was returning to Wales as I arrived in France, and why he was accompanied by a youth called Cagshaw, who must be a descendant of Gerbert's sister.

Was there a connection between the absence of Valérie and the presence in her villa of a British solicitor and conceivably a born heir?

I toyed with the idea of taking a taxi back to the Villa and forcing an entry into Gerbert's private apartments in order to seek clarification of such outstanding points. Instead, I channelled my impatience into a circuitous hike to the *vieille ville*, via a modern suburb clinging to the hillside, and bought myself another sandwich and some raisins and chocolate for lunch.

The show was due to begin at two o'clock. An hour or more before that, coaches crammed with majorettes and musicians in fancy uniforms arrived. The bandsmen and bandswomen who either were or were pretending to be soldiers organised themselves into military formations, and the girls pranced about, giggling and shaking their pompoms. Then big drums thumped, trumpets and trombones blared, piccolos tootled, and the parade down the hill, past the little square, the hotel, harbour and restaurants was rehearsed. Crowds of people had congregated by this time and lined the water's edge – cars were allowed to leave the cul-de-sac but not to enter it. People were selling silver balloons, foam guns, hot dogs and popcorn, and overgrown rival rabbits, a brown and a grey one, were collaring children in an attempt to persuade parents to pay for instant photographs.

A distant fanfare announced the first part of the festivities. Now the majorettes marched downhill in step and with synchronised saucy gestures, flourishing their long legs. Bands followed, the music of the Germans in metal helmets clashing with that of the orientals' cymbals and triangles, and the wind instruments of the French with the tin drums of the Caribbeans. When the marchers had gone by and come back, and been clapped and cheered, everybody turned to face the sea. Boats motored gently and were rowed from behind the harbour wall in order to be seen in all their glory. They had become floating bowers of flowers, vessels composed of mimosa, floral jokes, here a big fish made of wire mesh and carnations, there a motor car in shades of green, celebratory fantasies of early spring, invocations to nature to be kind to those who plough the earth and the waters, sacrifices to the gods who were chasing winter away and might be summoning warmer weather and richer pickings.

The boats were navigated inshore and their passengers started to throw the flowers to the people. They were five or six yards from the embankment, moving very slowly, and the wives, children and friends of the fishermen were chucking the mimosa in particular across the gap – some was caught, the rest fell into the sea. Excitement ruled, a good-humoured competition to catch the largesse of flowers was in train, hands reached out, screams and laughter mingled. The boats turned in the harbour and repeated the exercise in the other direction, and so it went on. The fish was robbed of its flowery scales, the car was dismantled and reduced to a framework of wire. The mimosa had been distributed, individual carnations were being tossed to and fro – boys were pelting the fisher-folk with them. But the carnival mood persisted, happiness was the order of the day, families were leaving the scene of the festivities with armfuls of flowers; and although I had entered into the spirit of the party as best I could, my thoughts were still fixed on the state of Gerbert's health and on mortality.

No one was about at the Villa Valerie, whether by accident or design. The gates were opened to admit me by remote control, and the front door was unlocked; but I did not meet whoever had done the controlling and unlocking. I could ask no questions, even if I would have been unlikely to receive any replies. At least those black cars had gone, either because medicine and law had combined to revive my employer or because they had failed to do so.

I went to my room and waited. My side of the house was in shadow, and the shade reaching over the lawn towards the convoluted trunks of the baobab was rendered ominous by a rising mist. Yet the knock on my door that I expected, the note cancelling the engagement of the evening, or the news that all was over, did not materialise.

At five forty-five, a quarter of an hour early, I descended the stairs and listened in the unlit hall. Not a sound emanated from the library – Gerbert could not be there. I walked in and was confronted by a scene that might have been a pictorial masterpiece, age and youth in suspended animation, the octogenarian with drooping head and rug over his knees, and the blackhaired girl whose white overall seemed to reflect the light from the single lamp on the desk.

The surprise was mutual – I was taken aback and they were roused or, metaphorically, brought to life.

I addressed Gerbert: 'I'm sorry, I didn't know you were here, I thought I'd be the first for a change – apologies for startling you.'

He smiled – the ghost of a smile crossed his countenance – and directed me to my chair by a minimal gesture of his head. Dark glasses and shadows combined together to hide his face, but I more or less guessed at its grey gauntness, and got the idea that his life was draining away in the form of words. He retained his dignity, however, and his voice, although faint, as if it came from somewhere farther away than the distance between us, had lost neither its music nor its magic.

'We should not apologise for startling each other,' he said. 'Half the aim of the artist is to startle. But the difference between art and journalism, art and sensationalism, is that the other half of the artist's aim is to delight. I must apologise for not being a delightful sight these days, and hope there's more to me than meets the eye.'

I reassured him.

'Thank you for your tact. The truth without tact is abominable – crimes without number, especially in art, have been committed in the name of so-called realism. All the same, as we grow older, the truth looks always more lovely, for lies both deliberate and ignorant are the bane of existence. The trouble is that you and I dealt in fiction and told the truth by fabricating stories, and now's the time for me to try to stick to the autobiographical facts.'

I asked him if he felt up to it. I asked how he was feeling.

'Lucky,' he replied, 'because my body's disintegrating before my mind. But the word "mind" is riddled with ambiguities. I meant simply the ability to frame and to speak rational sentences. "Mind" can also be used to describe those two very different faculties, cleverness and intelligence. I was a clever boy, clever enough to pass exams, win prizes, rise socially and satisfy my mother. I'm not boasting, I'm convinced that the exercise of my cleverness by overworking it had an inhibiting effect on any intelligence I might have had. And although there have been a few good writers who were much cleverer than me, it's intelligence coupled with imagination that writes the best books.

'I say with regret that I was not stupid to exploit residual Anglo-Saxon prudery. I jumped on the bandwagon – or should I say joined the gravy train? – by discussing our physical functions more frankly than the last pseudo-study, novel, article in the tabloids or television programme. I was in the avant-garde of the sexual revolution, I was the liberals' hero, and up to my neck in money. It was easy – it's always easy to strike gold if you're prepared to prospect for it in the sewers.

'But sex isn't everything. I mean, of course, that sex is everything until you have had enough of it. Sex is a finite resource of love, marriage, life and literature – there are a limited number of positions in which fornication is feasible, and time robs the act of some of its attractions. In the course of my career I found, first, that materialism as literary subject and theme is a dead end; and secondly that I could not stop butting my head against brick walls. My imagination was being stifled in its confined space, while I wondered what else I could write about, how I was to break the pornographic habit, and publishers, agents, fans and my bank manager egged me on and threatened me with the direst consequences if I deviated.

'The money cut both ways. I liked it – I tried to avoid the evil of loving it. A steady income is a great comfort, and capital can be a joy for ever. Whereas literature is lawless, money is subject to immutable laws – you know where you are with money provided you treat it right. I discovered the Stock Exchange and flirted with Mammon. At one moment I had to borrow my sister's savings; but I learned from my mistakes and as a rule chalked up more gains than losses. And I wrote better with money than without it – that I never starved in a garret may be a criticism of my work. The downside of my new riches was that I was additionally afraid to interrupt the flow of cash into my coffers.

'No doubt you know I married more than once. I was a mother's boy, and became a ladies' man. But my perfectionism came between us – or was it my promiscuity? I soon needed to earn in order to pay alimony as well as to keep myself in the style I was growing accustomed to. In other words I was caught in the jaws of the trap that is called success. My idealism was corrupted. I no longer believed that sex was the answer to any of the questions I began to ask myself, yet had to continue to say it was – as the salesmen of art never tire of telling us, you vary a winning formula at your peril. I wrote more and more books bearing the names of girls, who repaid less and less of the costs of their counterparts in real life; and I bridged the gap between income and expenditure – at least in theory – by speculating instead of investing in the market.

'And I reached the end of the road in artistic, emotional, social, financial and nationalistic terms. I had run out of literary steam, had nothing to write about, and was at an age when I could call it a day without loss of face. I was sick of women, on the verge of bankruptcy, and not particularly proud of my knighthood – I should have liked to believe that I deserved it. I had to reorganise my finances, and realised I could never do so in a country where I seemed to know every citizen and to be obliged to spend time and money on most of them. Moreover worse books than mine were now the rage, and I was unwilling to live in a decadent country where the mob sets the cultural criteria.

'That was when I met Valérie.'

Gerbert spoke with unwonted harshness and started to cough. To what extent the weak coughing affected the harsh speaking was not clear to me. His paroxysms were painful even to watch – I was embarrassed, averted my eyes, half-expected to hear the death rattle.

Marie was trying to help him, standing between him and me and bending over. She uttered unintelligible words of comfort, or comforting noises, in a high-pitched whisper, and moved her arms in such a way as to suggest she was administering pills. I said I would leave him in peace, but he succeeded in asking me to stay put – 'One moment!' At length he stopped coughing, and after a pause Marie poured the wine and knelt at my feet, proffering the tray. For once, as I thanked her, she raised her eyes to mine, and I thought I saw signs of strain and anxiety in their black depths – her eyes were large by oriental standards. Gerbert was able to accept his glass of wine shakily, and he returned my toast to good health with a wan sceptical smile.

'Forgive me,' he gasped after taking a sip; 'forgive me for repeating myself. I've been going over the autobiographical ground already covered in my book *Self Portrait*.'

I believe I pleased him by saying I had read it; also by promising he had never bored me.

He coughed again, drank a little more wine, and inquired with difficulty in a hoarse croak if I would object to a brief recess.

Not at all, I replied. We agreed to reassemble after I had dined. I then bowed out of the room so as to give him a chance to recover, be silent, receive treatment or struggle into the wheelchair.

It was sad, his melodic voice giving out like that, I reflected during the interim in my bedroom and in due course in the dining-room. I minded more that he had lost his voice than that he might be losing his life, and I tried to recall the sound of the sentence that must have strained his vocal chords, the peculiar rasp of his reference to his wife. The cause had been mechanical, I was persuaded – people often spoke in such loud runaway accents before sneezing.

I returned to the library apprehensively. He had recovered – he startled me once more by looking as if he had regained control of everything. He sat upright and dominated the scene. His subtle hint of a smile and the scarcely perceptible inclination of his head were welcoming. He resumed without delay, and his voice seemed to run on oiled wheels via my ears into some core of my being.

'The outward manifestations of love reserve their poetry for youth. In a perfect world without the modern media, a veil of discretion would be drawn across the loves of middle age, and geriatric passion would be hidden from publicity and prurience.

'Consequently I must excuse myself, since I'm about to betray some of my own matrimonial secrets. I do so to cut a corner, an allowable device when time is short, and because true confession carries more weight than stories in the third person, and because *Self Portrait* requires an epilogue.

'Nevertheless I feel the need to apologise. Too many "I"s on a printed page never pleased me, and now I'm sorry to inflict a rash of them on your long-suffering self. I would also like to add my regrets that you have not met my wife to hers that she has not met you.

'I was saying, before nature interrupted, that when I had written a respectable number of books, divorced more women than most men, made and lost more money, and become a knight in name if not in character, I joined the band of English artists past and present who have shaken from their feet the dust of a native land over-populated by philistines. I rejected responsibility and inclement weather and travelled south, where I was warm and not too many people knew me. My active life seemed to be over, and I settled not for contentment but for a modicum of comfort.

'One of the common denominators of love is that we're surprised by it. However well we know the ropes, love's validated by being different and by the coincidences that bring it about. Valérie and I met at a large lunch party in the house of mutual acquaintances. Neither of us had wanted to go; we did not like our host and hostess; and we were not in the mood for mindless frivolity – she was scarcely out of mourning for her husband, I was in mourning for my life. Besides, we had both reached the point at which normality ceases to search for romantic encounters. We had no wish to disturb the peace arrived at after more and less emotional skirmishing.

'They say that women can tell at a glance whether or not they could ever love a man. I'm not so quick off the mark, although I would claim to be an exception in that I prefer the company of the opposite sex – Welshmen resemble the English inasmuch as they're either in awe of women or else treat them like dirt. We were introduced. I approved of her looks, manners, clothes, cleanliness. She displayed the energetic cheerfulness of the female representatives of her race. I was placed next to her at the dining-table and we immediately crossed the borderline between conversation and communication.

'Her only marriage had been happy, I gathered. She had two adult sons, who lived with their respective wives and children in the ancestral home of the family in northern France. She agreed to meet me again. By then she had read one of my books – and as everybody knows art is a great seducer. We spoke of friendship; but I remember our saying *au revoir* and the handshake during which the old inimitable electric current passed between us.

'She attracted or, rather, charmed me increasingly. Beauty is indescribable – ask any author! – we all take pot shots at it and invariably miss the target. She seemed beautiful to me, and the more so because her features and expressions that I gloated over, that tugged unexpectedly at my heartstrings, were the inconspicuous sort, guarded by modesty and given significance by character.

'How are potential lovers of a stranger to recognise his or her qualities and defects that are not on show? The answer may be the acid test of love: not only by means of experience and hardheadedness, but simply by loving, we analyse and understand our better half. From a masculine point of view and for men of all ages, curvaceous flesh, dazzling teeth, a sensual temperament and a forward personality are wasting assets in comparison with dependability, kindness, good humour, patience and punctuality. In the fullness of time common sense is drawn neither to women who have had relationships with Tom, Dick and Harry, nor to their male equivalent.

'I declared my feelings too soon. I was taking a terrible risk; but in view of my hopes and intentions it would have been a mistake to let her regard me as no more than a friend – the gap between friendship and love can become unbridgeable. That she agreed to reciprocate was a compliment and a relief, or, to put it another way, a last throw of the dice so far as I was concerned.

'Our home has been this house. We lived in luxury in the Villa Valerie without any money worries. She had means of her own, and I was rich when I wasn't poor – I was still playing the market in those days. Fortune favoured us, and the sun shone on our love and our leisure.'

He broke off. He coughed as before and was tended by Marie. I waited in my chair – I was getting used to these interruptions, these pauses in which he regrouped his vital forces, and was reluctant to desert my post perhaps against his wishes. Moreover I suspected that the next part of the story would be his peroration, the conclusive summing-up of our symposium, and I did not want to miss a word of it.

Five, ten minutes passed. His coughing turned into a moan at one moment, and at another Marie's high-pitched whisper urged something, no doubt that she should be permitted to call in the doctor. He made negative noises, however, and at last with a thin white hand he propelled her aside, so that he and I were again face to face.

I had been relieved to think we were about to recommence. But the sight of him more than startled me. For the first time, distressingly, he had removed his black spectacles, and his small old eyes glittered with unnatural brilliance and were fixed on mine although I was not at all sure he could see me. And his thatch of grey hair was disarrayed – he looked like a different person, and his voice when he spoke had a new resonance – the idea crossed my mind that it came from another world.

This is what he said.

'Can we be happy ever after? Even a bad writer can suffer from divine discontent. I digress – I was going to give you a recipe for love in the twenty-first century. Belatedly, and if you'll pardon the mixed metaphor, my heart has seen the light just before it stops beating.

'The woman I love has been my education. She has presided over the revolution that wrought the essential change in me.

She taught as if by flashes of lightning, although never by storms. She's the inspiration of the philosophy of which you will shortly be in full possession, and what credit I take is only for loving and therefore learning from her.

'The lesson according to myself is pragmatic and derives from my personal experience. It does not chop logic, is neither academic nor excessively abstract, and is therefore not philosophical in the derogatory sense of the word. More accurately, it should be called *A Guide to Loving*.

'I'm old; I've issued no public statement for more than twenty years; I'm an obscure beachcomber and expat – why then do I imagine my opinions are worth broadcasting and might be of general interest and usefulness? The short answer is that I'm used to pleasing yours truly. My vocation has stirred after its long sleep, and I feel the need to right the wrong of my former views if I can. But my motives are also less selfish. By common consent this twentieth century is the cruellest known to history. In terms of quantity, at any rate, more people have suffered from man's inhumanity and specifically from his politics than ever before. What the politicians responsible had in common was a top policy of hatred. They said they would save the world by destroying certain classes of people and by conquering other countries and by genocide. Since their messages of destruction and death proved popular, and hate won the day and is still doing so, it must be time for every survivor of the carnage, and everybody hoping to live and die in peace, to reconsider the alternative.

'Love is a cliché. It's become a synonym for sex, a euphemism for lewdness, an excuse for bad behaviour, a dirty word in a pop song. It was never precise, unambiguous, self-explanatory. Books complicate the issue: they make out it's both monogamous and polygamous. What does it entail? Is it a sort of friendship, is it marriage – and how does one love someone else for ever, and why?

'My response, and the justification for talking to you as I have done, is that love's like charity not least in that it begins at home. Millions perish because things have gone wrong with the breeding and birth of tyrants. We are all winners or losers owing to the sexual partnerships of our forebears and parents. We are lucky if our mothers willingly bring us into the world, unlucky otherwise, especially if they have us aborted. I repeat that when mothers agreed to kill their unborn babies with the connivance of scientists and politicians, it was a black day for love.

'Loveless women produce hateful people: such generalisations may be denied by the unpredictability of nature. Yet a good home, happy parents setting understandable moral standards, plus regular meals, give the best of all possible starts and exert a beneficial influence on our future. We are less likely to treat our children worse than our father treated us.

'As for the rest, I have to refer to my recent discoveries. The guide to my guide of love differs from the other women and wives I've known. The essential and inclusive difference is that she's not an egoist. She's never held my seniority against me. She's not short of willpower, but never noticeably superimposes her will on mine. She is susceptible to reason, and refuses to argue the point, or, most importantly, compete. She asserts herself by gentle suggestions and soft words, by tact and intuition. She believes in silence and, although she's prepared to play her part in the outside world, that love requires privacy and the night in order to grow and flourish. She has her flaws – she's human – but, to my knowledge, no faults which are beyond my power to tolerate.

'She has persuaded me, she's demonstrated, that what's wrong with modern love is over-development of the ego. The catastrophic watchwords for today are "me too" and "why not?" All that I've told you would have been another set of stories with happier endings, but for egoism. Personal ambition, carried to extremes, ruins love, marriages, divorces and the lives of children; and, in the worldly context and politically, wrecks nations and makes war. The rebels who want it now, and demand to know why they should not have it, and trample people underfoot to get it, are the villains of the piece; the heroes and heroines seek happiness at no one else's expense. Animals behave better than we do, even if they eat one another: they play a team game with their species and never produce a leader prepared to exploit and sacrifice large numbers of his fellows to suit himself.

'The ultimate lesson I've learned re-emphasises the connection between love and death. With apologies for re-stating the obvious, to love is to hand over a hostage to fortune; and only idiots forget that fortune has a nasty habit of doing away with hostages. Beloveds die like flies in literature, operas and real life, and the joys of love are transformed into sorrows. My muse, my Egeria fell deathly ill, and I despaired. But she consoled me instead of the other way round. She was a model of unselfishness, and an exemplar of the courage of altruism. She urged me to keep my feelings for her in proportion, and explained that we both had to be ready to exchange the present for the future.

'In the blessed calm of her recovery I grasped the point that she had let me into the secret of loving without too many tears. Notwithstanding her commitment to our little world, and to her family and interests, when the call came she was immediately willing to answer and obey. Of course she had her religious faith, she always felt she was poised between earth and heaven, therefore which destination awaited her mattered less than might have been the case. Anyhow, somehow, she passed the highest of all existential tests and showed it was possible to resist fortune's threats.

'I would like to bypass arguments with heartless and hopeless atheists and help people to see what I have seen. Not mystically but practically I remember the readiness of Jesus to be crucified, the act called our "salvation" by wise men and women for two thousand years. The Christian message was endorsed as it were before my eyes: only by being prepared to renounce the best can we be happy in spite of circumambient danger and the prospect of pain.

'For death can win no victory if you refrain from fighting for your life. And life is the sweeter for remembering it is only on loan. Of infinite benefit to love is acceptance of the fact that you cannot possess the beloved, and that you share him or her with fate. You have to try harder to merit and retain affection. You have to renounce egoism, and be ready to bear bereavement.

'My love nearly died, and she and death between them resurrected me. I suffered a sea-change in my thinking, and my literary instinct directed me to communicate my thoughts to yourself, who might pass them on to others. If people were to read your account of the six evenings we have spent together, and to profit from my experience, they might seek above all to love and be loved. Consequently, one day, since love yearns to learn, education will abolish ignorance, and girls will be careful and boys will respect them, and sex will be subject to self-control and healthy babies will be born, and husbands will be kind and wives faithful and children brought up to follow in the straightforward parental footsteps. And love will overrule the politicians, and nations renounce quarrelling and bloodshed.

'Thank you for your attentiveness. You will be hearing from my man of business. Goodbye.'

Arrival and Departure

The next morning began with a difference not only because I was leaving the Villa Valerie later in the day.

Mrs Lee was not alone in the dining-room when I came down to breakfast. Lee and his brother were there, and all three were excited, huddled and chattering together, and none of them took any notice of me. I coughed and the group split up. But Lee and Mrs Lee bustled through the service door without a glance in my direction, and the gardening Lee provided an explanation in the following words, 'Madame soon,' accompanied by an imitation of an aeroplane in flight and by a grubby finger pointing at the clock. My deduction that Lady Aucott was flying home and would soon be landing at Nice Airport was reinforced by the appearance of the Mercedes speeding down the drive – Lee must be going to fetch her. I watched the car through the dining-room window while waiting for my croissant and coffee – it skidded as it turned on to the main road.

As a result I was seized with impatience to get out of the house. The alarm of the staff had been infectious; moreover my feelings were mixed – my curiosity to meet my hostess notwithstanding, I was shy of submitting myself to the judgment of such a paragon. I felt unworthy, as well as homesick, and bolted my breakfast and escaped to St Jean.

John of St John waved me to the telephone at the end of the bar and I spoke first to the airport people and finally to Grace.

The indispensable preliminaries over, I said: 'She's descending on us, her ladyship, Valérie.'

'What do you mean? Descending from where?'

'Probably from heaven! Gerbert talked about her yesterday evening as if she was a goddess. He claims she's the good woman whose love has introduced him to morality and changed his life for the better. He says she's the only begetter of his sonnets on the subject of love, which I'm meant to put into prose and transmit to the wide world.'

'If she's so good, why hasn't she been with her husband this last week? You're not so old or so ill as he seems to be, thank goodness, but I don't like to let you out of my sight. Where has she been? Where's she coming from?'

'Gerbert hasn't told me.'

'And how long has she been away?'

'I've no idea. But he doesn't grumble, quite the opposite.'

'Well, I'm suspicious, to say the least. Aren't you?'

'Yes, although I don't want to be involved in complications. Listen, I tried to get a seat on the midday plane. I'm longing to leave here as well as to be back with you, but no luck, I've had to book on the evening flight. I'll catch the first available train as soon as I reach London and take a taxi from our station – please don't even think of driving to meet me – I promise to ring you in an emergency or if it's too late for taxis.'

'Patience isn't my virtue, but I'll do my best.'

'Same here – I wasn't sure when or if Gerbert would finish with me, otherwise I would have booked in advance – sorry! And the timetables of modern travel are as vague as they were in the eighteenth century.'

'What are your plans today? How are you going to fill in till this evening?'

'I don't know – wish we were together here, as I have all along.'

We spoke of Oliver and of Crystal, who watched and waited by the front door for me to return. Then a coach-load of French pensioners burst into the bar. I could hear nothing except their demands for refreshment, said the equivalents of *au revoir* to Grace and *adieu* to John, and strolled back via the esplanade towards Villefranche, where I had thought of passing the time of day.

The way led me down the road with the entrance to the Villa Valerie. Through the great gates and behind the trunks of the baobab and the veil of its dangling fibres I could see cars, not just the familiar Mercedes, also a white van with odd markings, which I realised with a start was an ambulance. I had been absent for about a couple of hours, and Gerbert must be ill, probably dying, and my reluctance was replaced by the feeling that I could not as it were pass by on the other side.

My sense of crisis was aggravated by the lack of response to the entryphone: as a rule a member of the Lee family had pressed the button that worked the electronics of one gate without delay. At my third attempt to gain admittance a voice crackled through the loudspeaker. I thought it was female and speaking French, but was taken aback – the Lees had never used that part of the system – and answered in English. I spoke my name and added: 'Can I come in?'

She, the female at the other end who was not Mrs Lee or Marie, cackled back ungraciously in her francophone version of my native tongue: 'Who are you? What do you want?'

'I've been living in the house, I've been working for Sir Gerbert,' I replied.

'How are you working, what are you saying?'

'If you'd let me in I could tell you. I'm flying back to England today and need to pack and collect my belongings. Who am I speaking to?'

There was a pause, and the gate swung open.

I walked through the shadow of the baobab and started to cross the lawn as if by the stepping-stones of questions. Who was the aggressive stranger? Surely she could not be the angelic one? What was going on? Where were the Lees?

The answer to the last question materialised before my eyes. From a door on the left hand side of the house, the tradesmen's entrance, Lee and his brother, the latter now in a civilian suit, not in horticultural gear, emerged with bulging suitcases and were followed by Mrs Lee carrying an enormous parcel under one arm and with the other supporting Marie, who was crying and almost collapsing.

They were on the drive, at some distance from myself. They

looked like refugees, like one more picture of the twentieth century in action. I waved at them, I was loath to approach them, to march into the middle of all the linguistic difficulties, intrude upon their obvious misfortune and be inquisitive. The two men hurrying and stumbling because of the weight of their suitcases either did not notice or deliberately ignored me, while Mrs Lee vouchsafed none of her smiles, glanced darkly in my direction, shook her head with disapproval – or was it despair? – and giving a sort of hoist to her two burdens, her parcel and her daughter, tottered on.

As for Marie, her crying was as extraordinary as the rest of her behaviour had been. She had exchanged her reserve for abandonment. She drooped, she wailed, she resembled a rag doll, she no doubt clung to her mother although she seemed to have no strength in her body – it was painful to behold. Had she been physically injured? Who would hurt such a harmless pretty girl? What had happened? They passed me by, and I turned to watch them traipsing towards the gates, which moved mysteriously to allow them through and into the road.

I again headed for the front door. I could not stand and stare and worry and wonder any longer – someone might be waiting to admit me. But when I was within a few yards of the door it opened and, after a young man had stepped out, slammed shut.

The sequence of these events was confusingly abrupt. The man was twentyish and blond, wore an open-necked shirt and jeans, looked flustered and embarrassed, and I believed I had seen him before.

'Hi,' he said.

I introduced myself, but he showed no sign of recognition or interest. He gave an impression of adjusting to and recovering from a shock.

I asked: 'Why are the Lees leaving?'

He replied with an irritable lift of his shoulders: 'They're not the only ones. It's chaos in there,' and he jerked his head at the house and raised his eyes skyward.

'I'm just going in,' I said.

'Well, I didn't shut the door in your face – I won't be blamed for that – I've done nothing wrong, whatever some people think.'

'I wasn't blaming you, but I wish you'd put me in the picture. Don't we know each other?'

'Do we? I'm Jim Cagshaw.'

'Cagshaw was the name of Gerbert's sister, isn't that right? I saw you a week ago at Nice Airport – you were with Mr Curry, weren't you?'

'He's inside now – Mr Curry's our solicitor – they're all inside squabbling, the solicitors and doctors – I've had enough of it!'

'Were you here last week?'

'Yeah – and had to catch a plane at five o'clock this morning to get back – but Uncle's past it – what a waste of cash!'

'Is Gerbert dead?'

'He nearly pegged out before we arrived. We flew to Genoa and picked up a self-drive, but the traffic was wicked.'

'What about Lady Aucott?'

'She flew to Nice and pipped us.'

'She must be terribly upset if he's dying.'

The youth laughed or rather barked and answered in the ironical vernacular.

'Not half she isn't – so's everyone else, and Uncle most of all – but she's done the upsetting!'

The front door opened again and Mr Curry stood in the doorway and addressed young Cagshaw.

'I've been looking for you. I never thought you'd be outdoors. Come in!'

'No thanks! She kicked me out and I'm staying out, that's flat!'

Mr Curry wore the dark three-piece uniform of his profession. But the legal manner had deserted him. He was flushed, testy and officious, held a handkerchief with which to mop his bald head, and was neither cautious nor confidential. He also ignored me – and in spite of getting used to it I decided to draw attention to myself.

'Mr Curry, we met at Nice Airport last week.'

He looked blank for a moment, then came to, remembered who I was and how to behave, apologised, shook hands and explained: 'We're having a great deal of trouble.'

I said: 'I hear he's very bad.'

'Bad?' Mr Curry queried sharply. As if on second thoughts, having caught my drift, which had not been his, he agreed in a dismissive way, 'Yes, yes, I fear so,' and again called to Cagshaw: 'Please don't make matters worse by taking umbrage. You may be needed at short notice.'

'I won't go far, I'll be getting a bit of suntan,' Cagshaw replied with a touch of offhand humour and walked round the corner of the building in the direction of the sea.

Mr Curry muttered: 'It's his own funeral,' adding for my benefit: 'although I suppose that particular phrase applies elsewhere at the present time. Are you coming into the house?'

I said I was, and referred to my exchanges with the female on the entryphone.

'That would have been her ladyship,' he commented, using the last two words sarcastically rather than with respect.

We were in the hall, now rendered gloomier by medical equipment, spare flasks of oxygen and a TV set that might have been a cardiac monitor.

'What exactly is happening?' I inquired. 'I wish you'd tell me.'

He led me towards the door into the drawing-room, the extension of the library, from which the sound of male voices issued.

I hesitated and asked who the men were. The last thing I wanted was to be dragged into a lawyers' powwow. I pointed at the empty dining-room on the other side of the hall, where no member of the former staff would disturb us. But Mr Curry was disinclined, he gripped my elbow and pushed me in the direction he at least desired.

Monsieur Kolnatsch, in the library side of the room, was sitting in the chair in which Gerbert had aspired to make everybody happier. His colleague, equally black-haired and beetle-browed, occupied the chair I thought of as mine. They both aimed hostile stares at Mr Curry, while I received non-committal nods.

We sat on the seat in the drawing-room bay window and conversed in undertones.

Mr Curry's somewhat garbled explanation reduced to the following: Sir Gerbert and Lady Aucott had spoken to each other on the telephone late last evening; as a result the gentleman had immediately contacted his solicitor in Wales and demanded an urgent meeting, and the lady had issued a similar summons to her French solicitor; this morning she was the first to arrive at the Villa Valerie, Sir Gerbert thereupon had a heart attack, the lawyers and the doctors turned up together, and now for alternative reasons they were all waiting. The young man, he tacked on as an afterthought, was James Cagshaw, the grandson of Sir Gerbert's sister Queenie, who had died many years ago.

Could we, I inquired after thanking him for the information, go back to the beginning? How had it come about that a solicitor from Aberystwyth had written to offer me a job on Cap Ferrat?

'Sir Gerbert had invited me to stay at the Villa Valerie, I wrote to you as he instructed, and the letter was posted here.'

'Really?' I objected. 'Did you travel from Wales to the South of France to receive his instructions?'

Mr Curry lowered his voice still further. 'There was another matter he wished me to deal with. My firm has acted for his family for a long time, although he's had recourse to a local man of business since he chose to live abroad.' He gestured with his eyes behind his glasses at Monsieur Kolnatsch. 'He invited me here mainly to make his will.'

I had to laugh.

'At his age wasn't he leaving it a bit late?'

Mr Curry permitted himself a fleeting smile before appending the crucial adjective: 'A new will.'

'I see,' I said.

Actually I had already guessed that money alone would have persuaded three lawyers to keep a quarrelsome vigil at a deathbed.

Mr Curry fidgeted and fussed, glanced over his shoulder and inclined his head closer to mine.

'I'm speaking in strictest confidence,' he hissed into my ear. 'The last straw would be an accusation of professional impropriety. But I believe you're writing something for or about Sir Gerbert, and I feel sure he'd wish me to put you in possession of the facts.'

I calmed him down and encouraged him to continue.

'I drew up Sir Gerbert's will in Wales, and brought it back for him to sign. The two witnesses were Sir Gerbert's doctor – Docteur Palin, who's one of the team attending upstairs – and his physiotherapist. Jim Cagshaw was with me, but he was barred from witnessing the document. On the day we flew home to Wales we met you briefly at the airport.'

'Was Jim barred because he was a beneficiary?'

'Precisely.'

'The new beneficiary?'

'Possibly he would have benefited to a minor extent from Sir Gerbert's previous dispositions.'

'Didn't you draw up the old will?'

'No, that was done locally.'

'By Monsieur Kolnatsch?'

'Yes.'

'And Jim was left more in the new will than he had been in the old?'

'Yes.'

'How much more?'

'His great-uncle has been extremely wealthy, unusually wealthy for a literary man if I may say so, but I'm not aware of the present state of his finances. He has told me he was no longer interested in money, and he's been living an expensive life.'

'Whose large or small share of the spoils will Jim be getting? Who was cut out of the old will?'

'Lady Aucott has two sons, who both live in the medieval

chateau that belonged to her first husband's family, their father's family, since time immemorial.'

'Do you mean they're the losers?'

'I understand that Lady Aucott has been disappointed on behalf of her sons. Those old houses are very costly to maintain.'

'You amaze me. Was Sir Gerbert in his right mind when he changed his will? Considering his feelings for his wife, I should have thought that dead or alive he'd do absolutely nothing to displease her. Didn't they discuss the changes?'

'I think not.'

'Well, how did she discover the disinheritance?'

'You touch a sore spot.'

'I'm sorry – why?'

'I needed to ascertain if the legal requirements of the UK had validity in France. After leaving here with the signed and witnessed copy of the will, I wrote to ask advice of the colleague now sitting as he acted, behind my back. '

'Are you referring to Monsieur K.?'

'I am. We had corresponded occasionally. A legal letter is not so clear a guide to the character of the writer as a book is supposed to be. I wrote in good faith, and asked the relevant question in general terms.'

'And he sneaked to his client?'

'She must have been notified yesterday. She telephoned Sir Gerbert yesterday evening and told him she'd be arriving here first thing today. When we arrived on the scene, the doctor and the ambulance had already been sent for. Apart from sacking her staff and having words with Jim and myself, she's remained at her husband's bedside ever since.'

'Is he dying?'

'It's a coronary thrombosis, I gather.'

'She'll be desperate, poor woman.'

'No doubt.'

'I was thinking of asking what you're waiting for, and likewise Monsieur K., but the question might be considered morbid.'

'Oh no, far from it – you could say we're waiting for the

opposite of demise. The hope is that he'll recover sufficiently to sign his name.'

'On another will?'

'Either one drafted by the persons in the library, a will that probably reinstates the former beneficiaries, or one that I myself typed last night and brought with me. Because Sir Gerbert feared he'd be in hot water today, since Lady Aucott had found out that he favoured his family rather than hers, he wanted to have a final will handy, a compromise, offering a more equitable division of the estate. He also hoped that Jim Cagshaw would soften the lady's heart, but unfortunately in vain.'

At this point in our dialogue I decided to escape. I would steal upstairs, pack, decamp, and spend the rest of the day in the peace of Villefranche instead of in a narrow no-man's-land between warring factions. I therefore thanked Mr Curry for his presentation of the problem, and explained that I had already said my goodbyes.

'Not that it matters,' I could not resist adding, 'but last night, shortly before the telephone conversations you've mentioned, Gerbert was winding up his exposition of what was wrong with the world and what could save us all from eternal damnation with his description of his marriage. I can't square the praises he sang of his Valérie with a plot to treat her or hers shabbily. As soon as her back's turned he deletes her sons from his will, yet tells me how deeply indebted to her he is. The moral of the story seems to be that even the oldest husbands get into trouble if their wives leave them to their own devices for a few days.'

'Oh but Lady Aucott,' Mr Curry returned, 'left Sir Gerbert two full years ago.'

She joined us. That is to say the library door was flung open and she burst into that side of the room. Her desperation took the unmistakable form of fury.

She had been crying, but her eyes flashed fire. She looked sixtyish, whatever her age. She was below medium height, had a trim figure, and must have been blessed with that pretty combination, blonde hair and brown eyes. She was now vaguely fair-haired with chemical assistance, and her haircut was short and chic. She was elegantly dressed in a frilly silk shirt and a grey skirt, and wore pearls and lots of rings on her manicured fingers.

We four men rose to our feet, the three lawyers expectantly. She pointed at me and beckoned with an imperious gesture.

'You must talk to me – please come,' she said.

I followed her doglike, or at least as dogs are meant to follow, across the hall and into the dining-room.

'I'm very sorry about your husband,' I said to the back of her head.

'He is senile but obstinate,' she replied in her sullen Frenchified English. 'He is being tiresome, and I am exhausted. I shall see if those wicked servants took all my coffee.' And she pushed through the service door and stalked into the kitchen, self bringing up the rear.

She filled a kettle, turned on gas, opened tins and jars, cursed, clattered crockery and took no notice of me.

'Shall I say goodbye, Lady Aucott?' I inquired. 'I'll collect my things and perhaps you'd kindly work the front gates to let me out.'

She interrupted her activities as if with exasperation and demanded forcefully: 'What are you writing? Mr Curry' – she pronounced the name Curie, French-style – 'confirms that you work for my husband. What does he want you to write? You should listen to me, not to that dishonest man. Are you a journalist?'

'No, thank God!'

She ignored me.

'You want scandal? I shall present it to you. Sir Gerbert, the English knight with a foot in his grave, paid for a little girl to sleep with him. It is true, the girl Marie was sold by her parents. They turned my house into a brothel. Yes, this house belongs to me – did he tell you he was the owner? He lied again – it is mine, it was mine – I permitted him to live here, but not to make dirty love in my marriage bed. You think he was too old for sex? He was virile – my God! – and old men can do different things to young women. As soon as I returned this morning I dismissed those criminals. At least I am glad the Lees have gone – and I hope gone to the bottom of the sea!'

I held my peace although I longed to disagree. Marie did not merit such a description. I remembered her care of Gerbert and her extreme modesty, and then her sincere flood of tears in the garden. I was sure money did not enter into her relations with Gerbert, and was far from convinced that sex did. Furthermore, why was Lady Aucott so nasty about him when he had been so nice about her?

After fiddling with the coffee apparatus she rounded on me and resumed: 'Another thief was trying to rob me, that English boy – I locked him out before he stole my purse. With your Mr Curry he has made my husband leave him money that was mine by right. They conspire with somebody who is mad as well as old and bad. If necessary I shall fight in the law courts. Now, Gerbert will have to wake up and sign his name for the last time. The doctors order me not to worry or hurt him, but they don't know how much he has hurt me and my poor boys.'

The coffee reclaimed her attention, and I chipped in: 'Mr Curry is not mine in any sense, I scarcely know him.'

'He says he writes to you.'

'He wrote me a single letter on behalf of Gerbert to offer me a job.'

'What was the job? Why were you picked for it?'

'I'm a literary colleague of your husband, I too have novels to my name, and he wished to discuss material for another book with a fellow-writer, and thought I might be able to paraphrase and get his ideas into print.'

'Was he speaking against me?'

'Quite the contrary – he was making a philosophical statement.'

She shrugged her shoulders and scoffed: 'What did he know of philosophy? That is preposterous.'

'He was propounding a theory of love.'

'Oh no! How can he dare to do it? Have you read his old

books? They are immoral. They are disgusting. And think of his history – so many broken hearts!'

'He told me he had changed, he had evolved into a different person, and wanted to leave a record of his new view of the world.'

'Did you believe him? He does not know the meaning of truth.'

'Yes, I believed him.'

The kettle boiled. She poured water on the coffee grounds in a special jug and turned to challenge me.

'Well, what did he have to say?'

'He thinks love's dying out, and therefore we're all going to die. He talked to me for four or five hours for six evenings. I'm afraid I can't put his argument in a nutshell.'

'It's not difficult to say we're going to die.'

Her scepticism and sarcasm were harsh and, I felt, wide of the mark.

'He meant our species is decadent and fated, our religions are in tatters, we've lost the will and the ability to love one another, and we'll compete and quarrel and fight and bomb ourselves into extinction. He puts the blame for the cruelty of this century on the breakdown of personal relationships.'

She laughed bitterly and commented: 'He is an expert. In that respect he knew what he was talking about. Will you have coffee?'

While she poured it into two cups I explained: 'He generalised and then gave examples. He thinks science is the repository of all our contradictions, our creativeness and our destructiveness. His opinions would have been even more depressing if he hadn't had such a beautiful voice.'

'Please, sit down,' she urged me after she had seated herself on one of the rough wooden chairs around the kitchen table. She sipped her coffee as if for strength, and asked less furiously and with more objective interest: 'How did he generalise?'

'He's against abortion. He thinks mothers teach us the first lesson of love, and that women and mothers in particular are love's priestesses and guardians. That any or all of them allow their babies to be aborted represents our rejection of our highest capabilities and our signal to nature that we've failed and have become expendable.'

She interjected in a sort of passionate aside: 'Why don't those stupid doctors call me?'

I apologised for saying things she was not in the mood to listen to.

'No, don't stop – I would like to forget for a moment! So,' she continued, 'my husband blames women. As usual he thinks everything is the woman's fault. Probably he also told you we must save the world and how we must do it?'

'Yes, he did. I could explain later. Wouldn't you prefer to be upstairs?'

'The doctors said I was killing him, but it was more the other way. Please!'

'He wants women to be virtuous and renounce the folly of imagining they should or could behave like men. He wants men and women to re-establish and respect the connection between sex and the birth of children.'

'He wants a lot. How do you say it in English? He has had his cake and now he wants to eat cake. He is a hypocrite, he says all this and he has done all that – and it is too late for conversion.'

'Of course I hardly know your husband, and wouldn't dream of arguing with you. Nevertheless, may I suggest that he was logical in his concern for aborted children? He called them "sacrifices to our selfishness", and he convinced me at least that legalised abortion for no good reason does remove the cornerstone of the whole edifice of love and charity. And I can see what he meant by saying that one day those dead children will rise up and be the death of the rest of us.'

She jumped to her feet and began to harangue me. She was extremely agitated and marched to and fro on the farther side of the kitchen table, gesturing and sometimes slapping her hands against the sides of her head.

'He has deceived you, he has tricked you with his voice and his beguiling words – you are his victim as I and many others were. In the years of his strength he had no care for the children of whom he was or might have been the father. He was too impatient, I can assure you. He had no pity even for the son he recognised, and did not attend his funeral. And now he disinherits his step-children! He has broken his promise to me and my sons, and his word of honour – can you be surprised that he has driven me almost crazy? After I have given him so much he steals from me! He has no soul, you know. He has sold his soul. If you believe in him, you are in league with his master. Remember – whatever he has told you, when or if you write it down, your hand will be held by the devil!'

We were interrupted. The three lawyers stood in the doorway. A fraught pause ensued – I suppose it was momentary, but one of the men should have settled the question uppermost in her mind without delay. It was left to her to ask it.

Tentatively, quaveringly, in accents of sweetness I had not heard before, she queried: 'Is he . . . Is he ready for me?'

They affirmed that he was.

She turned to me. Her face was transfigured. The haggard look had gone, and the scowl and the anger in the eyes. They had been replaced by a blush and an expression of almost girlish hope and eagerness.

'When is your plane?' she inquired in a rush.

In the late afternoon, I replied.

'Stay till then! Don't leave me!'

They all went upstairs. I was on my own on the ground floor, and, although Gerbert's bedroom was nowhere near mine – in fact I never knew exactly where it was or how to reach it – I could not bring myself to go and do my packing. If or when Gerbert died, I might be needed. Besides, I was moved by events and their potential outcome, or at any rate curious, and the lady's plea was irresistible.

I suppose a quarter of an hour passed, during which I returned via the dining-room and the hall to the drawing-room-cum-library. Through the windows I saw Jim Cagshaw standing on the terrace with his hands in his trouser pockets and staring out to sea. His pose was defeatist – he looked like a man who was about to lose a legacy.

Monsieur Kolnatsch and his assistant came downstairs, talking together with animation and evincing no signs of sorrow. Mr Curry followed them and, unlike the others, who had pretended not to see me standing in the open drawing-room doorway, stopped and broke the news that Sir Gerbert was no more.

We exchanged expressions of regret, and in reply to the question I asked as soon as decency allowed he revealed that the will that compromised had been signed.

How had agreement been reached so quickly considering everyone was going to be disappointed?

'Lady Aucott withdrew her objections, and there was no time to waste.'

What about Monsieur K., who had just passed me by looking as pleased as punch?

'He'll administer the estate,' Mr Curry explained with a look that meant the administrator would be the last of the interested parties to lose any money. 'But what the estate amounts to remains to be seen,' he continued, permitting himself a professionally jealous smirk. 'I trust you will receive your fee of ten thousand pounds,' he concluded by way of a kinder afterthought.

He bade me a hasty goodbye, gave me his card, said he would have to inform Jim Cagshaw of the outcome, and that they had a long drive to Genoa to catch their flight back to Wales.

'Who's opening the gates for you?' I called after him.

'Lady Aucott's seeing to the remote control,' he returned. 'I gather she'd prefer to be alone.'

Two of the three cars disappeared behind the baobab, and Docteur Palin came downstairs and shook his head at me and climbed into his car and drove off. Then the ambulance men in white suits, carrying and collecting their equipment, took their leave.

I should have gone too, I decided belatedly. Valérie Aucott

had instructed me to stay, but that was before Gerbert died. Although I had no inclination to intrude upon the widow's grief and was alarmed by the prospect of having to console her, I had missed my chance and was now virtually imprisoned until she chose to release me.

It turned out differently. She joined me in the drawing-room – I had not heard her on the stairs. She was calm, clearly sad but dignified, and she invited me in a voice with a poignant catch in it to sit with her out of doors on the long chairs under the pine trees.

We arranged ourselves side by side, looking out at the sea that still twinkled unconcernedly, and when I had mumbled my condolences she said: 'What were the examples of love he gave you?'

I did the best I could. I cut it all short. Gerbert had described the dangers on the path leading to love's heights, I said. He began with marriage to a feminist, who made everybody miserable, herself included.

She shaded her eyes with a beringed hand.

I asked her: 'Shall I go on?' – and she nodded.

'Gerbert's argument was that the most important things in our world are personal relationships. Fame and wealth, also mundane failure, are trivialities in comparison with one person's wish and effort to be close to and good to another, in a word to love; and he thought fashionable modern art and philosophies and inventions were the enemy of loving and ultimately of our species.'

'What were his other examples?'

'Somebody called Caroline died of not knowing what sort of man would suit her. In the next example a French woman, married to a man who's at once dependent on her and mentally cruel, is driven towards adultery. Marriage loomed large throughout – Gerbert thought love was best served by the matrimonial conventions. He drew a depressing picture of adultery in the longer term. And he saw peril in permitting love to lose its sense of proportion. Finally, he spoke of the sorrows of parting that overhang love's joys. You were the heroine of his last story.'

'What did he say about me?'

'He said that thanks to you he could boast of an unusual feat. At a late age he had changed his ideas – also his character, he hoped. And when you were ill you taught him, your attitude forced him to realise, that the absence of egoism is the most lovable of qualities. Your unselfishness was an object lesson, and you presented him with the key to personal happiness and universal peace.'

Her initial reaction was disbelief. She turned to look at me as if to check that I was serious. Then with mingled wonder, humour, pride and wistfulness she asked: 'Did he really say those things?'

'Yes, I promise you.'

'I'm not like that,' she remarked. 'I never was.'

There was a longish pause.

'It's nice here, isn't it?' she began again.

My answer was enthusiastic.

She informed me: 'My sons were born in this house. We lived here in the south until my father-in-law died, my first husband's father, then we moved into the big family place.'

'Gerbert didn't buy the Villa Valerie for you?'

'Oh no,' she laughed. 'He only changed its name, and mine too – he robbed me of my accent. Did he speak of our marriage?'

'Not in detail.'

'I was a widow when we met. He was renting an apartment in St Jean. I was lonely and he was not happy.'

'He had already retired from writing, I believe.'

'Oh no. He would have written if he could. He was blocked, he was old – and it was not good. But he never meant to retire. His work was his life.'

'But he loved you.'

'Oh yes – how do you say it? – in his way. And I loved him in another way. His personality was formidable, you know, and he was a bit mysterious. Always there is romance in rescuing and being rescued.'

'Gerbert was or had been extremely successful and had many more years to live – may I ask what you rescued him from?'

'He was poor, not rich. He had spent his money on wives. But I had enough for two. What mattered more was that he disliked himself. He was disillusioned and he wished to reform and write a better book. Every woman would love to be the inspiration of an artist.'

'Well – now in principle you are.'

'While we were together it was difficult. Every day he worked in the library, but he only filled the wastepaper basket. He would not write, he could not, unless he was pleased, and he was never pleased and always more frustrated. He tried again, he tried to do other things, and nothing was good, and he said he could not go on. But I was the one who did not go on. After I was ill I could not bear to return to the Villa Valerie. I have spent the last years with the doctor who cured me – he laughs and he loves me! Gerbert and I were better without each other. Now he has found the words he wanted, and you will change them into a fine book. You are a writer, you will have guessed what he was telling you.'

I must have looked blank, for she elaborated.

'His first wife was a foolish feminist. I think he was saying sorry to all the women in his life. He loved too many and made them unhappy, and he was not wrong to remind people of the problems he had created. But he was born to tell stories – and he was like the oyster, for him real life was the grain of sand. He could not say directly "Forgive me!" Instead he has given you his best pearls, and you will rearrange them in a beautiful pattern.'

'Your attitude to your illness enabled him to spin the best pearl – he spoke movingly about it.'

'I wasn't so very ill.' She shrugged her shoulders and said: 'Perhaps I became part of the dream that was his art. Tell me, did you make friends with my husband?'

'Our association was more professional than friendly. He was politeness itself, and won my respect, but he used up all his energy in talking to me nonstop for hour after hour.'

'Talking of personal relationships, which, frankly, were more in his mind than his nature, he had no friends – only one woman at a time to love. That was why women loved him. Also we were tempted to compete with literature, which defeated us.'

'Will you tell me something?'

'Maybe.'

'What else was Gerbert working on in the barren years?'

'He worked for money. He had a little money, and I was paying the bills. He was a clever man and he invested cleverly. He grew rich – it was his compensation for the poverty of his writing, you see. At one moment he had millions. But I heard he had changed his will, and I was worried that he was not well and might have done something unkind.'

'You spoke to him on the telephone last night, I believe?'

'He told me that he was leaving his money to his relation instead of to my sons. And I told him no, you cannot, you have broken your promise, you owe me your money for letting you live in my house and for supporting you, and we agreed that in your will you would repay me. We had an argument. I was angry and said I would come at once to Cap Ferrat. And I found my husband was sleeping with that unprincipled girl. I did not mean to make him ill by saying he was cheating me and by throwing out his servants.'

'Please accept my sympathy.'

'But then it was wonderful. I am happy as well as sad.'

'May I ask you to explain?'

'Oh yes. I wish you to know, and he would have wished you not to be mistaken. Just now, when I returned to our bedroom, I held him in my arms. We both said we were sorry – and he whispered in my ear, "Money not important, except it has brought you back." I was so happy, we were so happy, to be reunited.'

A pause followed.

She said: 'The wills are not the point. My husband was right. Whatever he has arranged will be good for me.'

Strange, I reflected in another pause: the shrew of earlier in the day was tamed, and displaying some of the qualities attributed to her by Gerbert, who had put the absence of egoism at the top of his list of aids to love.

Touchingly, and right or wrong, she added: 'Please pass on his message. Because of it, because of the effort of conveying it to you, he shortened his life. If he ever belonged to the devil, his services to love have set him free.'

Coming Home

I think I can understand Crystal's barks. When I stepped out of my taxi at midnight I heard the intermittent half-bark half-growl which she utters without leaving her basket in order to warn us of odd sounds and suspicious activities. The click of the latch of our garden gate was a more serious matter: she must have jumped out of her basket and was barking for all she was worth, barring entry and threatening an intruder with blue murder. But she recognised my step on the paving stones and the way I turned my key in the lock, and desisted, listened and then voiced that rumble at the back of her throat expressive of affection, of emotion at least, followed by the yelp of excitement.

Although I pitied the neighbours whose peace might have been disturbed, I have to admit that Crystal's vocal greeting was music to my ears.

And Grace was waiting with open arms in the hall.

Our dog knows her place and respects our priorities. She paced the floor with flattering impatience, squirming and wagging her tail, until we had greeted each other, and immediately seized her chance to stand on her hind legs and rest her front paws on my shoulders, gaze into my eyes and give the side of my face a lick.

The sweetness of home never cloys, personally speaking. With whom you share your home makes a big difference, of course. To shut the front door and find myself on the right side of it is to be released from the strains of modern travel in any direction and for any distance, of avoiding enemies and strangers with uncertain tempers, of trying to remember the names of acquaintances and even of friends, and of most of the problems inherent in what is euphemistically called an interesting life; while quiet harmony solaces ears that have suffered from the noisiness of today, and as a rule goodwill is on offer and – I am lucky enough to claim – everything else the heart could desire.

Moreover age has nothing to do with my anti-social attitude: I have felt the same ever since I married Grace.

In the next day or two we talked more than usual – silence is another of the customary comforts I enjoy and I hope she does. To start with I had to tell her I had changed my mind again – I could not possibly write Gerbert's book – and to explain why.

'I wouldn't be able to do justice to his monologue on the night before he died, it was such emotional stuff and he was so eloquent. He assumed, he insisted that I was to put his ideas into my own words – it was another of his peculiarities. I wasn't allowed to use a tape recorder. I jotted down a few notes, but only from memory, not in his presence – they're just reminders of the subjects under discussion. I couldn't begin to reproduce his subtle language. Even if I could I wouldn't – I wouldn't dare, because Valérie told me his stories are autobiographical, and some of the characters in them may be alive and kicking and disposed to sue me for libel. Besides, where does Marie fit in? Should I include or exclude her? The book would certainly be incomplete without a chapter on Valérie, who confided in me under pressure of her grief and won't want me to spill any beans. She'd take inevitable exception to being accused in print of causing her husband's death. For these reasons over and above the fact that I've retired, and struggled out of the literary vortex, I've decided finally not to be bribed to do Gerbert's dirty work.'

Grace may be the least materialistic person in the world, but is not a woman for nothing.

In the light of the above she put the following question to

me: 'Will you be paid for not writing some sort of an account of your time in France?'

I replied, 'Mr Curry stated categorically in his original letter that whether or not, or how, I used the literary material on offer was up to me. Not a single string was attached to the money, and no cancellation fee was mentioned.'

At other times Grace asked: 'You didn't have a word about the ten thousand with Mr Curry while you chatted in the library?'

And then: 'Will Mr Curry or Monsieur Kolnatsch be paying you?'

And again: 'Do you think Valérie's aware of the deal? Will her sons honour it? Or will the money have to come out of Jim Cagshaw's portion?'

On the metaphysical level she wondered why Gerbert had not expressed a forceful wish to be named as the author of his views of love.

I suggested: 'He identified with the unknown artists and craftsmen who built the Gothic cathedrals. He said something to that effect – I can't remember – he was refusing to re-enter the rat race for prizes – and renunciation was the ideal he urged us all to aim at. But his own idealism doesn't bear too close an inspection. What did he ever renounce? He must have known that I'm not a plagiarist, and would never pretend his views were mine.'

It was the month of March, in which the advance guards of spring skirmish with the retreating forces of winter. Our northern weather was not the equal of those sun-drenched days on the Côte d'Azur, the golden dawns, the unruffled sea, the star-studded skies at night. We burned our store of logs with prodigal abandon in order to keep warm and in hopes that the wind whirling over the estuary would abate, the rain and hail cease to drum against our wedged windows, snow fall elsewhere and our plumbing reject the attentions of Jack Frost. Sometimes we were not disappointed. Coolly, fleetingly, the sun kissed the landscape, and promised to do better soon. Crouching perennials and green shoots as it were raised their heads from slit trenches. We would mystify Crystal by donning the footwear, overcoats, scarfs, gloves and hats that she had no use for, and up on the moors would be encouraged by getting hot for a change.

We discussed life and death in the Villa Valerie, and swapped Grace's first and my second thoughts.

For example, Gerbert's last whisper into the ear of his wife was much more ambiguous than she had chosen to believe. Money was not important, she reported he had said, except that it brought her back: was the sentence celebratory, as she supposed, or regretful? Was he pleased that they were reunited, or cursing because his testamentary arrangements had summoned her to do battle with him once again? Had he meant there was no important money left? That he was claiming to have used the will business to reclaim Valérie from her lover, the laughing doctor, was an incredible theory, since it depended on chance. If Mr Curry had not submitted a query to Monsieur Kolnatsch, a query unauthorised by Gerbert, and if Monsieur Kolnatsch had observed confidentiality in the matter, she would have been blissfully ignorant, and the will disinheriting her sons would not have come to light until the signatory was underground.

No, the gratification that Valérie owed to that sentence did not make sense. If Gerbert had wished to be reconciled with her, why had he not written or rung her up? He was not so foolish as to gamble that two solicitors would make such a wish of his come true by behaving not very well.

The likelihood was that he had been as ambiguous on his death-bed as ever, and that she had once more misunderstood him. He was indicating in a roundabout way that money and her love of it would be the end of him.

In this context Grace let her imagination run riot. Valérie wanted to recover money that was or was not hers by means of Gerbert's signature, and she was the owner of the Villa Valerie and a remunerative future patient of Docteur Palin whereas her husband was at his last gasp. What would be the medical treatment in such circumstances? A venal doctor might administer one of those drugs which can both bring about a temporary revival and hasten death.

More realistically and seriously, our joint scepticism focused on the relationship between the two Aucotts and Marie. Valérie's story was that Gerbert had slept with the girl, and, since Marie's parents and uncle should never have allowed so improper a conjunction, and possibly because of legal implications, she had sacked the lot. But how had Valérie discovered that the teenager was sharing the bed of a man about to die of old age? Even if geriatric men have been known to satisfy young women somehow or other, surely traces did not tell the tale? Besides, the bedfellows would not have been caught between the sheets, for Gerbert had known his wife was arriving, he had telephoned Mr Curry the previous evening and instructed him to rush out a peace offering of a will. Valérie's action was explicable in terms of propriety, legality, possessiveness, jealousy; but Grace's deduction was that the spring and source of the information that inspired it would have been Gerbert himself – he must have flung it at her in a quarrel.

We speculated, we disagreed and mainly agreed, we extended our enjoyment of our own little world, where we were together again, by peeping into the world of others, and trying to unravel the mystery of another marriage. Post-mortems are the best thing about social life in our estimation – not for us the party but the discussion after we have survived it – and in the present instance we were conducting a sort of post-mortem in every sense.

In the better weather out of doors we were distracted by the seasonal treats on view, we could concentrate on nothing but the exceptional sweetness of early springs in England, not so many more of which we would live to love. We conversed by means of that exclusive tick-tack only known to compatibility. The Villa Valerie began to resemble the setting of one of my novels or perhaps of one of the less sexual of Gerbert's; and indoors, especially on colder evenings as we huddled round the fire and provided there was nothing worth watching on television, we would reorganise my experiences behind the baobab tree as if they had been fiction.

But at length, some three weeks after my return, almost on impulse and possibly in search of grist for the mill of our deliberations, I telephoned Mr Curry.

He immediately raised the subject of my fee. He told me he had sent copies of his original letter setting out Sir Gerbert's offer and my letter accepting it, which taken together could be considered contractual, to Monsieur Kolnatsch, who was now in charge of the purse strings; and he was sorry both to say he had heard nothing from that person and to hear that I had received no communication.

He was not to worry, I urged him, because it was not my intention to earn the larger sum. The five hundred pounds I had already been paid, and the interest of my visit to the Villa Valerie, were more than adequate remuneration in the circumstances.

His disappointment that I would not be writing the book was complimentary.

He continued: 'May I remind you that no conditions were attached to the fee, and no deadline was set. Sir Gerbert was willing to pay for your judgment, whatever it turned out to be. You're generous not to press for payment. Nevertheless I feel responsible and must apologise.'

I tried to set his mind at rest, and reverted to the terminal events at the Villa Valerie.

The object of the will that became the bone of contention, I recapitulated, was to cancel a debt. Gerbert had the cash borrowed from his sister Queenie on his conscience, and decided that his stepsons were nowhere near the breadline and needed money less than his own great-nephew: was that correct?

Mr Curry assented.

But his plan misfired. The lady heard that she – or her family – was disinherited, and telephoned her husband to warn him she was flying south in the morning to reclaim her dues.

Mr Curry carried on from where I left off. Sir Gerbert then rang through to Aberystwyth and called for a will that compromised and the attendance of his solicitor and great-nephew at the Villa Valerie with the minimum delay.

'Was he frightened of his wife?'

'I would prefer to say that he required support and to be provided with an olive branch.'

'The olive branch of the will that split the money between his stepsons and Jim Cagshaw?'

'Exactly.'

'Which was meant to turn away the lady's wrath?'

'Yes.'

'Well – I'm disillusioned. Gerbert made out his marriage was perfect, and I've now discovered that he and his wife lived apart, and that she had a lover and was money-mad. What did she do to the poor old man to get him to sign on the dotted line?'

'It was Monsieur Kolnatsch who put the pen in Sir Gerbert's hand. She was begging her husband not to bother about the money. I was in the room at the time, and I heard her say she only wanted him not to die.'

I used to be the regular type of writer. Not for me the manic bursts of energy, during which good writers produce a book in a few months and bad writers in a day or two, nor the fallow periods, in some cases of years, that are apt to ensue. I have to plod along day in and day out, praying that my prose will not seem to readers to mimic my progress, and try not to miss a single five-hour stint – catching up can take me any number of extra hours.

Grace graciously consented not only to marry me, but to adapt to my habits of work. Even after I officially retired we have stuck to it, breakfast at seven forty-five, going our separate ways till one o'clock, a brief nap after lunch if possible, afternoons available for joint activities, early evenings of cogitation, writing letters, paying bills and telephoning to friends and relations, then with luck uninterrupted time together till the next day. Visitors are welcome, and the more so if they toe our line and appreciate our dog.

But we had no guests to stay in the weeks after my return from France – Grace had been careful to keep them at bay. As a result we were able to prosecute our inquiries into the case of the Aucotts without interruption.

Intermittently Grace made the following points.

'I'm probably just being feminine by having reservations about Valérie – women always suspect other women of not being so wonderful as men think they are. Gerbert contended that she'd initiated him into the higher philosophy of love, but I'm swallowing a big spoonful of salt. And Gerbert isn't easy to agree with in my humble opinion. He condemned abortion on demand and was all for renunciation; but heaps of women who have had abortions might like to say that for the best of reasons they'd renounced their chance to have a beloved child. He may have meant that if women get pregnant by mistake they ought to renounce their good names and their jobs and their free lives and devote themselves to their babies; but how hard that is! Was he right to expect women in trouble to be the martyrs of a new puritanism, when he hadn't renounced much, in fact nothing, and nor had Valérie? She deserted Gerbert to please herself, then was angry with him for taking a grandfatherly shine to his nurse. She wanted to be the proud possessor of both her husband and her doctor. I'm not polygamous – sorry! As for death – I'd rather not think of renouncing Crystal, let alone Crystal's master.'

In my cupboard of a study in the mornings, instead of reading the books I had never had time to read, and doing watercolours and drawing up horticultural plans, I nibbled at the edges of my promises in respect of retirement by scribbling a few random recollections on scraps of paper.

I never intended to write anything to speak of, but discovered that the farther my work receded the more I wished to be back amongst the problems of composition, the hard slog, the minor triumphs and more often the tragedies. I missed the double life. The habit of holding a pencil was hard to break, and the love of stationery seemed to be fatal. No doubt I was influenced by Gerbert's scoffing at the idea of retirement for a literary man, and I was certainly caught up in the web he had woven.

I kept on jotting down what I thought he had said before I forgot it altogether. While suffering pangs of regret because I had not taken notes at the Villa Valerie or recorded Gerbert's utterances covertly, and because I felt the burden of his argument was slipping into oblivion, I came to a contradictory realisation that the book I was tempted and taunted by was beyond me. Crucially, and setting aside the more obvious negative reasons, I was not at all sure that I knew the end of the story, or, therefore, the beginning. The darkness intensified the deeper I peered into it. The whole business was a literary fiasco. Yet I cudgelled my brain to remember what was said in those sombre evenings in the library. I pinned down themes and sentences as if they had been precious butterflies, and was haunted by the sound of a voice unlike other voices.

One day I reminded Grace: 'Valérie did renounce something. According to Mr Curry she tried to spare Gerbert the effort of signing his final will and testament. She was renouncing his money, which she might have believed was actually hers.'

But Grace was three times more logical than I had been, and replied: 'I can't believe she needed any more money. And she was only renouncing what would have belonged to her sons. And I bet she had heard the rumour that there wasn't enough in the kitty to make much difference to anybody.'

On another occasion I inquired: 'Why do you think Gerbert told me that Valérie did not hold his seniority against him? He was older than she was, but not all that older. It wasn't remarkably nice of her not to blame him for being old, but it would have been remarkably nasty if she had blamed him.'

In this instance neither Grace nor I could supply an answer.

Of course we had other things to talk about. We discussed Grace's brother and the dilemma he also posed.

Worries with regard to Oliver she had kept to herself while I was in France. Oliver's problem had not been solved in hospital: he was drinking too much as soon as he was let out, she now told me. He would not stop; although a bottle of whisky had broken his leg, figuratively speaking, he could not wait to buy other bottles and drain them dry; and when she implored him not to, he was displeased and the more impatient to get back to his hermitage which was tumbling down, damp, dirty and far away from shops. He was still on crutches, unable to drive for the time being, and would be dependent on neighbours he had insulted and ignored. Yet he rejected Grace's offer to spend a day a week replenishing his stores, cleaning, cooking and filling his deep freeze, and keeping him company.

His daughters had families to look after in Canada and Australia, and expected Grace to dance attendance on their curmudgeon of a father, who snubbed them on the telephone. His wife Marian had divorced him thirty years ago, and been dead for ten years, but he harboured resentful memories of her. He had hated his job in the Civil Service, and felt altogether hard done by.

Grace expressed her thoughts on the subject by referring to Oliver and Gerbert in more or less the same breath.

'My brother hasn't renounced a single thing – that's the truth, and that's his trouble. He started so well – I used to look up to him – and he was persuaded he was somehow superior – he believed he was better than he was. He's never got over his disappointing career, or his divorce, or growing old, or his girls not doing their duty to care for him. He won't change any of the pig-headed ways that are killing him. I'll try again to help, I'll soon try again, but meanwhile I am going to take no for an answer. He will – and he can – do as he pleases. Gerbert's talk of renunciation was too general a generalisation for me – it could mean that suicide's the finest flower of love. Where does the renouncing stop? Where does it turn into selfishness? But if only Oliver had been better at loving! Gerbert was right to say that everything, and probably all of us, depend on personal relationships.'

Grace also set in train the resolution of our joint preoccupation.

After a couple of months of speculating and scribbling, of guessing and not getting anywhere, she asked: 'Why don't you write to Monsieur Kolnatsch and demand your pound of flesh?'

'I don't know his address.'

'You could ask Mr Curry to forward a letter, or you could write to Valérie herself.'

'Forget it! Let's forget Gerbert!'

'But you don't forget, and nor do I. Couldn't we try to tie up the loose ends?'

'I'd rather not be under a financial obligation to write the blessed book – and then there's my promise to you.'

'Oh that! Your promise to retire was always conditional on mine to keep you happy and well. You'll have to have a shot at this book. You need to write Gerbert out of your system and I'm longing to read the full account of life and death at the Villa Valerie. Besides,' she added, notwithstanding her unmercenary instincts and in spite of knowing how relatively unremunerative my work had always been, 'sales of the book may compensate for all the money we're unlikely to be paid.'

Not for the first or – I hope – the last time, I followed her advice.

Then Crystal had another so-called turn. We were alone on the moors – Grace had dropped us there on her way to do some shopping and was due to pick us up at the same spot in an hour. Crystal caught sight of a rabbit in the middle distance and chased after it with overexcited leaps and bounds. She is a hopeless hunter, she would starve in the wild, far from stalking her prey she rushes at it loudly giving tongue, and a baby rabbit that once jumped into her mouth caused her a mild nervous breakdown. In the present instance the rabbit hopped at its leisure behind some gorse bushes and she swerved and skidded after it. She did not reappear. I called her and uncharacteristically she did not respond. I walked, then hurried to look behind those bushes and found her lying on her side in a grassy clearing.

I was sure she was dying or dead. Her eyes were shut, her nose dug into the grass – her position showed none of her natural elegance and indicated collapse. I felt sick at heart or simply sick. I spoke her name and knelt down beside her and tentatively touched her head, ashamed of myself for wondering if she had succumbed to a canine disease, rabies for instance, and was about to bite me. She did not stir, but I noticed she was breathing. I began to stroke her head and at last she gave another sign of life by ever so slightly twitching one of her black ears.

Slowly, it seemed, although in no more than three or four minutes, she recovered. In succession she opened her eyes, wagged her tail, licked my hand, yawned as dogs always do when they have to think – she must have been thinking about what had happened to her – and finally struggled to her feet. We completed our walk and met Grace as arranged. At the vet's, for we drove straight to the surgery, Tim West repeated his opinion that Crystal was okay and these slight fits of hers were not a cause for concern.

Crystal herself proved the point, she exhibited no ill effects. Grace was reassured, or said she was in order to calm me down. I was concerned nonetheless. It had happened so terribly quickly, whatever it was could have been lethal, and I loved that dog, she was my great true friend. The episode not only rammed home the lesson that irreplaceable wives and partners were always at risk, it reinforced the questions raised and perhaps answered by Gerbert.

Was the willingness to relinquish even our best beloveds – renunciation qualified by common sense – the ultimate piece of the jigsaw puzzle of the ideal of loving instead of hating? If so, and because the event on the moors inclined me towards Gerbert's way of thinking, I owed it to everybody – not exactly to him, he still owed me – to try to publicise his views, which could be helpful.

But the equivalent of the brick wall that still gave me a headache when I toyed with the idea of doing so had compressed itself into an inclusive query: why had Gerbert waited until Valérie left him to praise her virtues and elevate her to the status of almost love's presiding deity?

Even Grace had no answer to it. I reissued my reminder that Valérie herself had said: 'I'm not like that.' I repeated that Gerbert had seemed to me to be telling the autobiographical truth, although he was a writer of fiction. At length I elicited that most evergreen piece of wise advice: 'Wait and see!'

Mr Curry replied to my letter and enclosed two documents.

He began by apologising for sending me a copy of Monsieur Kolnatsch's response to my request for payment of my fee.

It – the first enclosure – stated in English not grammatical enough to quote that Lady Aucott's sons were considering a legal challenge to the will of Gerbert, who, in their opinion, had not been of sound mind in his latter years. Until advisory rulings had been obtained, the estate was not obliged to pay the outstanding bills for inessentials, and Lady Aucott was determined to resist pressure to accept responsibility for her husband's debts.

Mr Curry had another apology to make: he should have warned me long ago, even before I travelled out to France, that the ten thousand pounds could be problematical. Shortly after relaying the offer of such a sum, he explained, he had reason to suspect that Sir Gerbert was short of money to splash around, and omitted to warn me; but he asked me to believe that he had acted initially in good faith, and then in what appeared to be the best interests of his client and of the recipient of an invaluable literary legacy.

His second enclosure was a newspaper clipping that featured another letter. So far as Mr Curry could tell the letter was genuine. He hoped that I would understand it better than he did, and that it would shed not too intrusive a light and might persuade me to produce a record of my visit to the Villa Valerie after all. He also explained that Sir Gerbert as a son of the town remained a hero in Aberystwyth even if his name had lost some of its lustre internationally.

The journalist responsible for the article was called Jones and was the arts correspondent of the paper and one of Gerbert's obituarists. Jones' story was that the contents of the letter had been offered for sale together with a photocopy of the holograph item, a guarantee of authenticity, and, to prove there would be no complications over copyright, a list of the countries in which the document had already appeared. He had tried and failed to talk to the literary executor of the writer, Gerbert's widow Lady Aucott, in order to check that she sanctioned publication; but he had received assurances from her elder son by a previous marriage that she had withdrawn her objections for the sake of art and posterity. Although Jones could not identify the original owner of the letter or supply additional biographical information, he was proud to be able to bring it to the attention of lovers of literature in general and of Gerbert's work in particular.

'Dearest and kindest of all the women I have known,' the letter began. 'We must part. Disaster strikes tomorrow morning – and three would be unbearable company for me and I believe for you. What will happen, God alone knows!

'For letting me love you I cannot reward you as I wish to. The little that remains of my money is not my own, and if I gave you things in the house you might be accused of having stolen them. The best I can do for you, apart from the cash I trust you still have, is this piece of paper. Take it to Monsieur Jacques Sander at 24 Rue de la Victoire in Nice and say that I sent you. Monsieur Sander will translate my last fond words and pay you a fair price for them. The proceeds should get you and your family home to Indonesia and even provide you with an attractive dowry.

'Do not show the letter to Kolnatsch. Monsieur Sander is my friend and will be yours, whereas Monsieur Kolnatsch is in the enemy camp. Monsieur Sander will give you a copy of my letter to remind you how much I loved you and still do.

'Many years ago I turned my back on literature. Then you strayed into the desert of my existence. I was waiting for death when the miracle occurred of our creation of new life. The mistake I made, the crime I committed, the action I insisted on your taking and you took against your will and your instincts to please me, and your dreadful illness and my penitence and misery changed me. You forgave me, you redeemed me. I would have written it all down if I could. Instead I commissioned another writer to listen to me, to witness my change of heart, and, if he will, to edit my regrets and my receipt for happiness into a publishable text.

'You have sat at my side for the last seven evenings, you also have listened to me. Perhaps luckily you have not understood, yet I believe the tone of my voice will have conveyed my feelings for you. Our love is our secret – I would not expose you to the judgment of an envious unjust world. I had to attribute to another woman some of the beneficial influences you have introduced into the two years of our communion. But this evening, my seventh opportunity to plead the cause of love, after I had that coughing fit and lost my spectacles and nearly my life, I spoke exclusively of you – I could no longer bear to deny you. Your youth and the beauty of your body and soul, your generosity and your altruism are the sole source of my precepts for a brave new better world.

'Remember that I would have married you if, again, I could. I have spoken so much and so longingly of marriage because it was denied me. To consort and not to marry is a betrayal of love, and part of the conspiracy of men against women. Whether or not marrying me would have been good for you is not known – in those circumstances I might have lived too long. Anyway I swear by all that's holy that I shall love only you till I die.

'Now, believing as you have taught me to believe that the ultimate test of love is to renounce itself, to abide by fortune's treatment of the hostages we have given it, to mourn those precious ones who are taken from us without losing faith in life, I pray you will find a husband who appreciates your charms and virtues, and I promise if possible to rain blessings on your marriage and your children.

'No more – I am weary.

'Gerbert.'

Epilogue

One of the problems that loomed over the writing of the above was the fame or notoriety of the book's hero. Was I expected to whitewash, was I permitted to debunk him? And what would his wife, wives, relations, friends and admirers have to say? Would I be ruined by the awards of damages imposed by crass juries and crazy judges?

In the event the problem solved itself. The deeper I delved into the amorous and financial affairs of my cast of characters the more obvious it became that I could not reveal their real identities. My literary line never was to hurt feelings and cause offence – I would be a richer man if that was not the case.

The author or speaker of the major portion of this book remains incognito. It is probably not for me as his employee, colleague, ghost or accomplice to comment on the quality of his work; but I must say that after a century of unparalleled hate, a new look at love cannot be a bad contribution to the millennium.

He wrote to Marie, 'Our love is our secret' – a statement with which all genuine lovers will agree. To kiss and tell is to turn love into hot air. The tender plant of love wilts if you permit other people to touch it. I dare not be more descriptive of my own wife and our marriage than I have already been.

Fiction has therefore to some extent taken over from fact. Perhaps I have produced that contradiction in terms, a true romance. Although I would not presume to draw an odious comparison, Gerbert and I were alike in that we belonged to the peculiar tribe of novelists, we fitted into that mildly schizophrenic category, and felt lost without the extra life we were accustomed to lead through the characters we created. He returned to literature as he stood on the threshold of death, and, almost devilishly, tempted me out of my retirement.

I use the past tense advisedly. I have assured Grace that I mean to call it a day this time round. Autumn is now slipping into winter, but the other evening was warm enough for us to sit out of doors and watch the sun set across the estuary. Crystal sat with us with her head on my knee, and, to counteract wifely scepticism, I promised to add a paragraph to my book that would effectively finish my game of make-believe.

Here it is: I am not me, nor is Grace the woman I love who wears my ring on her finger. Our dog is not a German Shepherd called Crystal, and we overlook no inlet of the sea on which the evening shadows fall. The location of the house within reach of the moors, and the park in which the Villa Valerie rises through mist behind a baobab tree, are elements of the land of dreams where I have also lived and been happy.